Also by
Kimberly Willis Holt

Novels

Keeper of the Night
When Zachary Beaver Came to Town
Part of Me: Stories of a Louisiana Family
The Water Seeker

———

The Piper Reed Series
with Christine Davenier

Piper Reed, Navy Brat
Piper Reed, Clubhouse Queen
Piper Reed, Party Planner
Piper Reed, Campfire Girl
Piper Reed, Rodeo Star
Piper Reed, Forever Friend

———

Picture Books

Waiting for Gregory
with Gabi Swiatkowska

Skinny Brown Dog
with Donald Saaf

The Adventures of Granny Clearwater and Little Critter
with Laura Huliska-Beith

MY LOUISIANA SKY

KIMBERLY WILLIS HOLT

SQUARE
FISH

HENRY HOLT AND COMPANY
NEW YORK

Acknowledgments

I am grateful to each of the following people who helped me during the writing of this book: To Jennifer Archer, Ivon Cecil, Isabel Davis, Laura German, Alyce Joyce, Robin Quackenbush, Sue Walker, Chery Webster, Pat Willis, and Carol Winn, who read my manuscript and gave vital input. To my grandparents, Henry and J. P. Mitchell and Zora Willis, for helping with the details. To Linda Green of Rapides Parish Public Library, Mary Connell of LSUA's Bolton Library, and the staff of Amarillo Public Library, who helped me with the facts.

And a special thanks to my agent, Jennifer Flannery, who believed in this story early on, and to my editor, Christy Ottaviano, for her faith and vision of what this book could become.

SQUARE FISH

An Imprint of Macmillan

Library of Congress Cataloging-in-Publication Data
Holt, Kimberly Willis. My Louisiana Sky / Kimberly Willis Holt.
p.   cm. Summary: Growing up in Saitter, Louisiana, in the 1950s, twelve-year-old
Tiger Ann struggles with her feelings about her stern but loving grandmother,
her mentally slow parents, and her good friend and neighbor, Jesse.
ISBN 978-0-312-66095-6
[1. Parent and child—Fiction.   2. Grandmothers—Fiction.   3. Mentally handicapped—
Fiction.   4. Friendship—Fiction.]   I. Title. PZ7.H745My   1998   [Fic]—dc21   98-12345

Originally published in the United States by Henry Holt and Company
First Square Fish Edition: February 2011
Square Fish logo designed by Filomena Tuosto
Book designed by Meredith Baldwin
www.squarefishbooks.com

10 9 8 7 6 5 4 3 2

AR: 4.6 / LEXILE: 770L

This story is dedicated with love:
To Jerry, for always supporting and believing
in me; to Shannon, for bringing true joy and
meaning to my life; and to my parents,
Ray and Brenda Willis, who showed me the world
but taught me about my roots so
I'd always have a place to call home.

MY LOUISIANA SKY

one

Folks around Saitter don't understand why parents would name their daughter Tiger. But Daddy says it's because of love. Momma had a kitten named Tiger when she was a little girl. She loved that kitten so much, she hugged it too hard and it died. Momma wasn't going to let that happen again, so when I was born she was real gentle with me.

Some people in Saitter say Momma and Daddy should have never been allowed to get married because they're different. Folks around here call it retarded, but I like "slow" better.

Even though Daddy got through twelve years of school, most folks say teachers felt sorry for skinny Lonnie Parker. Just passed him from grade to grade like they do some of the basketball players. Momma never went to school, but Granny taught her to read.

With those kind of odds, I should be dumber than

an old cow. But I'm not. In fact, my classmates' parents are still scratching their heads trying to figure out how I got straight A's and won the spelling bee five years in a row. It's even harder for them to believe Momma taught me to read. But she did. Momma likes reading comic books. I read about Superman and Donald Duck when I was four. Now Momma likes me to read to her because I can read the words she can't.

❦   ❦   ❦

It rained every day the week after I finished sixth grade. The clouds hung low in the gray sky and the raindrops poured down, hammering our roof with a constant patter. But by Saturday, the day Aunt Dorie Kay came to visit from Baton Rouge, the sun came out in all its glory and the sky returned to a brilliant blue. When we heard her car drive up near the gate, Momma ran out of the house like a little kid. She grabbed hold of Aunt Dorie Kay so hard, my aunt wobbled on her high-heeled shoes.

"Whoa, Corrina." Aunt Dorie Kay caught her balance and smoothed her dark hair back in place.

"Oh, Dorie Kay, I missed you so much," Momma squeaked. She stepped back with her dirty bare feet, admiring Aunt Dorie Kay from head to toe. "You're as pretty as a picture in a fancy ladies' magazine."

Aunt Dorie Kay was Momma's younger sister. To me, she was the most sophisticated person I had ever known. Today she wore a tailored navy blue suit that matched her shoes and she smelled better than the perfume counter at Penney's. She wasn't beautiful like Momma. Momma's long dark hair fell to her shoulders, and her body curved in all the right places. But somehow Aunt Dorie Kay's flat chest and narrow hips appeared stylish in her pretty clothes. She wore more makeup than any Saitter woman dared to, except for the women who went to the Wigwam honky-tonk on Saturday nights. But while their faces looked caked on, hers looked glamorous.

Aunt Dorie Kay gently cupped my chin with her hands. "Twelve years old. Tiger, you are growing up into such a young lady."

Her voice was smooth like a deep, calm lake. I wanted to dive right in and let it work magic on me. Turn me into someone I wasn't. But as I looked at my reflection in her eyes I was reminded of what I saw in the mirror. I saw Daddy. He was tall and skinny with thin red hair and a long neck. His narrow eyes squinted when he smiled and his nose took up a lot of room on his face. But folks say kids change a bunch before they finish growing. Especially in the summertime.

In the afternoon my best buddy, Jesse Wade Thompson, stopped by to say hello to Aunt Dorie Kay. He and I were sitting on the living room floor, drinking Grapettes and listening to Elvis on the radio, when we heard someone drive up.

Aunt Dorie Kay leaned forward, causing our tweed couch to squeak. She drew back the calico curtains. "Why, Tiger, look. Are you expecting something from an Alexandria store?"

I rushed to the window. A Mitchell's Appliance delivery truck screeched to a stop in front of our gate. Jesse Wade and I dashed to open the screen porch door for two men carrying a bulky box. Two weeks ago we received a box of twenty-four baby chicks Granny had ordered. But this box was almost as big as our woodstove.

I held the screen door open for the men. "Excuse me, sirs, but do you have the right house?" Brando, our one-eyed cat, leaped from the swing and pranced off the porch.

The taller man with a harelip exchanged smiles with his stocky helper. "I don't know. Whose house is this?"

My breathing was hard and fast. "This is the home of Jewel Ramsey and her kin." Jewel Ramsey was my grandma. I hoped the box was for us, but I knew it had to be a mistake.

They carefully lowered the heavy box onto the porch. The harelip man wiped sweat from his brow with his handkerchief and dug out some folded papers from his back pants pocket. He unfolded a yellow slip, then slid his finger to the bottom of the page. "Well, let's see here. You say Jewel Ramsey and her kin?"

I hunched my shoulders. "Yes, sir. That's what I said."

He frowned and shook his head. "Nope. I don't see anything that says that."

My heart sank. "It's probably for your family, Jesse Wade." Mr. Thompson owned the plant nursery where Daddy worked. They could afford things that came in big boxes.

Jesse Wade leaned his curly black head against the doorway. "We're not expecting any deliveries from Mitchell's."

Aunt Dorie Kay walked onto the porch while the man continued to study the papers. He frowned, shaking his head. "Nope. This here paper says for the family of Jewel Ramsey *and* Lonnie Parker." The corners of his mouth turned up into a slow grin.

The other man laughed loudly and slapped his knee with his hat. "Fooled ya, didn't we?"

My heart felt like it flew plumb out of my chest. I raised my chin and stood straight. "Yes, sir, that's my grandma and daddy. Right this way, sir. Can I get you some iced tea?" The men followed me inside, carrying the box. It took up so much space in our plain little room.

Momma darted out of the kitchen with a half-peeled potato in her hand. The spiral peeling bounced as she ran toward the box. "What is it?" she asked. "What's in that box?"

"Hold on, Corrina," Granny said, walking slowly behind and wiping her hands on her apron. Her black hair was pinned in its usual tight bun, but some fine locks stuck to her full face. Aunt Dorie Kay stood near the window, smiling as she watched us.

Daddy, returning from the garden, clopped up the porch steps. He started to walk in, then looked down at his muddy boots, backed out, and pulled them off. He walked in the house with white socks on his feet, rubbing a dirty hand across his red chin. I couldn't tell if his face was red from the sun or because two strangers stood in our house. He studied the box, then shyly peered at the men. As always, he spoke slow and cautious. "What's this box doing in our house?"

"It's for us, Daddy. The men said it was for us."

The deliverymen headed toward the front door. The stocky fella tipped his hat and said, "You folks have a good day."

The screen door squeaked open and shut as I examined the puzzled faces in the silent room. I dashed out the door before the men reached their truck. "Wait a minute, sir. Who is this box from?"

The tall man opened the truck door. "It's on those papers we left with you."

I ran back to the house and grabbed a paper stamped INVOICE off the box. It said Doreen Kay Ramsey. Aunt Dorie Kay bought it! I whipped around. "Oh, thank you, Aunt Dorie Kay!" It was just like Christmas.

She yanked gently on my long pigtail. "Don't you think you better see what it *is* you're thanking me for?"

Momma's focus didn't stray from the box. "Open it," she demanded. "Open it, Lonnie."

We all stood around Daddy while he drew his knife from his front pocket and carefully cut into the box. Cardboard sides flapped to the floor and revealed an object I had seen only in stores and Jesse Wade's living room. Dark oak surrounded a wide green screen. A brand-new RCA television set!

Momma jumped up and down, squealing like a baby pig. Daddy stepped back, stunned, brushing the hair from his eyes as Jesse Wade whistled approvingly.

Then, as if we all planned it, everyone, except Granny and Jesse Wade, grabbed Aunt Dorie Kay and hugged her until she lost her balance and fell to the couch, laughing.

"Thank you! Thank you, Aunt Dorie Kay!"

Momma raced to the TV and stroked it like a puppy. "Thank you. You're the best sister in the whole world."

Daddy clasped his hands together, cleared his throat as if to begin a speech, and said, "This is mighty nice of you, Dorie Kay Ramsey. It must have cost you a whole lot of money."

Aunt Dorie Kay must have made a big salary working as a secretary in Baton Rouge.

Granny frowned, turned on her heels, and marched to the kitchen, her apron bow riding high over her huge hips. A hurt look spread across Aunt Dorie Kay's face as Granny walked away.

I wondered why Granny wasn't happy like the rest of us. There weren't many families in Saitter with a television set.

"It's a beauty," Jesse Wade said. "Make sure you put a lamp on top. Momma says that helps you see better. Speaking of Momma, I better get on home. She'll be hollering for me if I don't."

My eyes were so fixed on that TV, I hardly noticed him leave. Daddy plugged it in, then Aunt Dorie Kay helped connect the rabbit-ear antennas. When they finished, she asked, "Tiger, would you like to turn on the television?"

"Yes, ma'am." I turned the knob to the right. We waited and waited. Maybe Marlon Brando would be on TV. My knees grew weak from the thought of seeing his dreamy movie star face right in the middle of my living room.

Finally the screen lit up like magic. Soon we saw a man in black and white like some of the movies I'd seen at the picture show. His lips moved, but we couldn't hear anything. We stood there with our mouths open, watching the man talk. Aunt Dorie Kay bent down and turned another knob. The man's voice boomed from the set. "And that's the news for June 1, 1957."

Everyone but Aunt Dorie Kay jumped back. Granny started out of the kitchen, frowning with her hands on her hips.

"Volume," Aunt Dorie Kay explained as she adjusted the knob that lowered the sound.

Daddy and Momma exchanged puzzled glances. Then their faces smoothed out. Momma smiled and Daddy nodded with a grin.

Later the *Hit Parade Show* came on. Daddy settled on the couch, clapping offbeat to the music, while Momma and I held hands and danced around the living room. Floorboards creaked as our steps thumped against the wood.

Aunt Dorie Kay perched on the arm of Granny's lumpy lounge chair, her eyes glazed as if she were miles away from our living room. Every once in a while she batted her eyelashes.

While Momma and I danced, Granny entered and sank into her chair. She stared at the TV, but a film covered her eyes like the times right before she fell asleep in church. She and Aunt Dorie Kay seemed to be in worlds of their own.

Then Granny spoke. "Don't you have better things to spend your money on besides a noise box?" Last year when Granny learned Aunt Dorie Kay hired a colored maid to clean her apartment, she'd said, "That gal thinks money grows on trees."

Now Aunt Dorie Kay said, "Oh, Ma, lots of families are buying televisions."

Granny shook her head and walked back into the kitchen. Her large, lumpy hips reminded me of two fighting cats trapped in a sack.

I sat down and offered a silly grin to Aunt Dorie Kay. She smiled back, but her eyes looked sad. Granny's comments spoiled the gift for me, but Momma kept dancing by herself around the room.

two

Sunday morning Aunt Dorie Kay drove back to Baton Rouge. I stood in my nightgown on the porch steps, waving as she drove away in her green Ford.

Granny sat on the squeaky porch swing, sipping coffee. "Better hurry and get changed for church."

"I wish we could visit Aunt Dorie Kay in Baton Rouge. It must be so exciting to live in a big city."

"Hmmph." Granny's face pinched up like she had taken a bite of her famous sour pickles. "Ain't nothing exciting about not knowing your neighbor, driving in traffic, and breathing dirty air."

Granny seemed to resent Aunt Dorie Kay moving to Baton Rouge something fierce. She stood, walked over, and opened the screen door, then threw her coffee on the grass. As she looked at the sun rising over the pine trees she said, "This is God's country, Tiger.

You'll learn that one day. Hope it don't take you as long as your aunt to find that out."

I loved Saitter. I loved the longleaf pines that grew thick around us like a fort. I loved the smell of honeysuckle after a hard rain and the way a swim in Saitter Creek cooled my skin. But I didn't know what was wrong about taking a trip away from God's country now and then. Even God let his angels fly away sometimes.

Granny walked into the house. "Better hurry. We need to leave for church in twenty minutes. Corrina?" she called to the back of the house. "Are you still sleeping?"

"She's playing with the chicks," Daddy said.

"You better fetch her," Granny said, then she headed to her own bedroom.

Twenty minutes later I carried a buttermilk pie out to the truck. Once a month in the spring and summer our congregation spread quilts and blankets on the grass and ate dinner on the church grounds. Everyone brought a dish according to the first letter in their last name. *A*'s through *G*'s brought meat, *H*'s through *Q*'s—side dishes, *R*'s through *Z*'s— desserts.

Daddy met me at the truck with a bowl of string

beans that Granny had cooked for Momma to take. His hair looked dark and greasy from the goop he used on Sundays to make it stand up in a flattop, and he smelled like he'd splashed on a heavy dose of Old Spice.

"Uh-oh," he said, tilting his head to the right.

"What?" I asked.

"Rain."

"But Daddy, the sun is shining mighty bright, and the weatherman on the radio said it's a perfect day for picnics. And baseball," I added silently.

"Nope. It's gonna rain. Hear them frogs?"

Sure enough, the frogs' loud croaks bellowed around us. I had been too busy listening to the gospel songs on the radio to hear them.

Once when I was about five years old Daddy taught me to listen to the frogs as a sign of rain. We stood perfectly still with our arms stretched out like scarecrows and our heads tilted back. Soon we felt raindrops thumping on our faces and landing on our tongues. I learned Daddy was hardly ever wrong when it came to the weather, but today I had hoped he was.

"Yep," Daddy said as Granny and Momma approached, "the frogs are calling the rain."

Granny reeled around and headed back to the house. "I'm getting my umbrella. Lonnie's forecasts are better than my old bones." Granny said she knew when a cold front would blow in because she could feel it in her right arm where she broke it years ago.

Daddy learned the ways of the wind and rain from his daddy. Granny said Grandpa Parker was a wild man the way he camped on the creeks for months at a time while his wife and children survived on their own. Granny claimed that's what made Daddy's momma so cruel, raising young'uns by herself while her man lived on fish and animals he hunted in the woods. Every once in a while he returned home and brought his family a deer he had killed or a mess of catfish he'd caught. Sometimes he'd take Daddy back to the woods with him.

"If you watch and listen close enough, the earth talks to you," Grandpa Parker told him. He taught Daddy to notice how spiders build shorter and thicker webs before a storm, how frogs croak loudly right before a rain, and how grasshoppers chirp their loudest when it's hotter than the Fourth of July. Grandpa Parker knew how to breathe to the rhythm of the earth. That's why no one could believe it when he was struck dead by lightning while he fished in

Tanner Creek. The sheriff found him laying faceup in the water with a perch in his net. Daddy said he reckoned that was a mighty fine way for his daddy to leave this world.

❧   ❧   ❧

Sunday school was the best part of church because Mrs. Thompson, Jesse Wade's mother, was our Sunday school teacher. I loved to listen to her talk. Her people came from south Louisiana and she peppered her sentences with Cajun words like *Oh yea, cher!* which meant something like—Of course, sugar! She was lean, tan, and brown eyed, and she wore her short hair stylish like Aunt Dorie Kay. At church Mrs. Thompson always wore a hat, gloves, and a cross around her neck with Jesus on it because she used to be a Catholic. Our preacher, Brother Dave, said Catholics celebrated Jesus dying while Baptists celebrated Jesus rising from the dead.

After Sunday school I sat between Momma and Daddy, waiting for Brother Dave's long sermon. Brother Dave came down the aisle, greeting everybody. Before he preached, he leaned his broad chest over the pulpit and asked if there were any announcements.

Jesse Wade's daddy stood with his hat in his hand.

His bald head shined from the overhead light. "Brother Dave," he said, "I have a treasury report. We now have seventy-five dollars saved toward our new piano."

"Amen," said a few men.

"Amen!" Momma said so loud I felt the hairs prickle on the back of my neck. Granny frowned at her from the first row of the choir. I heard a girl giggle in the back of the church—probably Abby Lynn Anders, the prettiest girl in Saitter. We'd been in school together since first grade and we would be going to seventh grade in September. She had golden curls that bounced when she talked and laughed. I bet those curls were bouncing right now.

"Seventy-five dollars. Now that's wonderful news," Brother Dave said. "Wouldn't you agree, Sister Margaret?"

Sister Margaret sat behind the old piano, her rear end pouring over the bench. "Oh, yes, Brother Dave." She smiled at Mr. Thompson.

Mr. Thompson rotated his hat in his hands. "When we collect the offering momentarily, if you want any of your money to go toward the new piano place it in an envelope marked 'piano fund.' "

Sister Margaret began to play "Just a Closer Walk

with Thee" as Mr. Thompson and Mr. Hill passed around the offering plates. She winced every time a piano key stuck or clattered. I bet she chose that song because it showed the awful condition of our piano and reminded everyone to put more money in the plate for the new one.

Daddy reached into his pants pocket and pulled out his envelope. He handed it to me and I printed *Piano Fund* on top. Then he dug into his pocket again and pulled out some change to put in the regular offering.

When Brother Dave started to preach, I listened to each word carefully, but then he said something about lost sheep. And that got me to thinking about wool, which led me to thinking about my itchy winter wool skirt. At that moment I swear my knee started itching like I had been bitten by a bunch of mosquitoes. I started scratching, digging my fingernails into my skin so hard I was afraid I might bleed. All because Brother Dave said the word *sheep*.

By the time I started listening to him again I was as lost as those lost sheep. I had no choice but to start thinking about the baseball game I'd be playing with Jesse Wade and the other boys after dinner.

I stared straight ahead at the choir. Granny's eyelids lowered, then she opened them wide again as if to keep from falling asleep.

Just as I was daydreaming about hitting a home run, the preacher made some important statement and a few of the men said, "Amen."

"A-men," Momma said, fanning herself with a paper fan. Some girls in the back giggled again. Momma probably didn't understand a lot of what the preacher was saying. She knew her Bible, though. She could flip to Ezekiel as quickly as she could find Matthew.

As if things couldn't be bad enough, Granny's eyelids were now shut. Her heavy bosom rose and fell in a deep slumber and the corner of her mouth dropped open. Sure enough, a rattling snore escaped right after Brother Dave said, "Glory to God."

Momma jabbed me in the side with her elbow. "Did you hear Ma?" she asked. "That sounded louder than the eleven o'clock train coming down the tracks."

"Shhh!" I said, but it was too late. The congregation roared. Momma began to laugh too, only I don't think she knew they were laughing at her.

"That's right, Sister Jewel," Brother Dave said, smiling. "Glory to God!"

Granny's eyelids opened as quick as a shade raises. This time they stayed open.

Before long, the sermon ended and we sang "Just as I Am." I hoped nobody felt the calling to be baptized or share their testimony today. My stomach growled for the spicy smells drifting from the kitchen.

Some of the women had slipped out of church early to get the food ready and make the coffee. Other people must have felt the calling of their hunger too because no one walked down the aisle. Brother Dave stood in front of the pulpit, his Bible pressed against his chest, rocking on his heels. As the last verse was about to end he announced, "Let's sing that last stanza one more time."

Finally the closing prayer was said and everyone headed outside to spread blankets and quilts on the ground. The morning dew had disappeared, but the air was sticky. My skin felt like flypaper with every mosquito around Saitter sticking to it.

On one end of the table lay the main dishes—squirrel gumbo, roast, ham, fried catfish. Bowls filled with baked sweet potatoes, string beans, and black-eyed peas squeezed in the center of the table. Desserts were at the end—buttermilk pie, blackberry pie, lemon cake, and fig cake.

I ate so much my side felt like it could split open. When I'd taken my last bite of Granny's buttermilk pie, Jesse Wade came by and asked if I wanted to play baseball.

"Take your Sunday shoes off first," Granny said.

"Yep," said Momma, "take them shoes off." She was already barefooted, sitting on our quilt with her legs stretched out in front of her.

Suddenly six-year-old Jack Savoy ran by and pulled Momma's hair. She sprang up and raced after him.

"I'm gonna get you!" she called out. Two other little boys chased her.

Under a gray sky I played baseball with Jesse Wade and the boys, but I couldn't help but watch Abby Lynn and the other girls—Dolly and Annette and Jackie—sitting on the sidelines. Their full skirts spread out on the blankets like opened umbrellas. Abby Lynn's charcoal gray felt skirt had a black piece of fabric shaped like a record on the front.

I wondered why they didn't want to play ball. The older girls played on the school softball team, and I was looking forward to trying out next year. Maybe Abby Lynn didn't want to mess up her Sunday clothes and combed hair.

I wanted to sit with those girls and be a part of their secret world. I wanted to know why they laughed when nothing seemed particularly funny and how to bat my eyelashes like Abby Lynn. When I fluttered mine, someone always asked if I had something in my eye.

Bobby Dean raked his comb through his slicked-back hair, spat on the ground, and pitched me his hardball. I smacked it head-on and took off for first, second, then third base, not stopping until my feet touched home plate.

"That a way!" hollered Jesse Wade.

Behind home plate, I glanced at the girls. They were clearly unimpressed, staring at me with blank faces. Then I did something I thought I would never do. Right there in the middle of the game, I quit playing. If I was ever going to be friends with Abby Lynn and the other girls, I had to start by not playing dumb games with the boys.

"Where are you going, Tiger Ann?" Jesse Wade asked as I walked away from home plate. He slipped off his catcher's mitt. "Is something wrong?"

"Nope, I just don't feel like playing anymore."

"Huh?"

"Aw, let her go!" Bobby Dean yelled, probably relieved that he now had a chance to win the game.

"Come on, Tiger," begged the boys on my team.

It wasn't fair to them but I kept walking, wondering what the girls would think of me now. I walked by them real slow to give them a chance to ask me to come over and sit with them. I smiled at Abby Lynn, but she looked down and frowned at my dirty bare feet. My stomach fell straight through the ground.

I walked back to our quilt, where Miz Eula was talking to Granny. It was hard to say which was more pointy on Miz Eula—her nose or her chin. Today she reminded me of a sharpened number-two pencil with her yellow dress and skinny ankles leading to black shoes. A heavier woman would surely have broken those ankles just by walking.

"You see, Jewel," Miz Eula said, "I'm not nosy, but people tell me things and what am I supposed to say? Tell them to shut up? So anyway, Miz Smith was telling me about her up and leaving—"

Granny listened with her eyebrows raised and one corner of her mouth turned down.

"Hi, Tiger," Miz Eula said. She turned back to Granny. "Well, as I was saying, Jewel—"

"My gracious!" Granny shouted, jumping to her feet. "What has that child got into now?"

Daddy carried Momma in his arms, racing toward Granny. Momma's face was all puckered up.

"I was chasing those boys through the woods," whined Momma, "and I stepped on a splinter. Please don't use a needle to get it out. It'll hurt something awful. Please don't!"

I was thankful the girls were watching the boys play ball on the other side of the churchyard.

"Better go," Granny said. "Nice to see you, Eula." She yanked the quilt off the grass.

"But I wasn't through telling you what I heard from Miz Smith."

The sky thundered.

"We'll have to do it some other time," Granny said, folding the quilt. "Right now we need to git home and tend to Corrina's splinter."

People grabbed covered dishes, blankets, and young children. But the thunder didn't seem to faze Miz Eula. She followed Granny toward the truck. "But I'm almost at the good part."

"Good-bye, Eula," Granny said.

Momma, Granny, and Daddy got inside the pickup just as fat raindrops fell from the sky. I hopped into the back, holding the umbrella. As we drove away I looked at the baseball field. Abby Lynn and the girls picked up their blankets and rushed toward the church, but the boys kept playing ball. I heard Jesse Wade call out, "Strike!"

I was feeling torn into two giant pieces. Part of me wished I was inside the church with Abby Lynn, helping her dry off those golden curls, and part of me wished real bad that I had stayed in that game and struck out Bobby Dean.

three

Monday was laundry day. Granny put red beans in her gumbo pot while I pumped water from the well. On the back porch, I poured the bucket of water into the washing machine, dumped in a cup of laundry soap, and turned it on. *Ker-chunk, ker-chunk, ker-chunk.* The sound of that machine and the crisp smell of soap powder made my fingers raw thinking about the stacks of clothes I'd be feeding through the wringer.

Momma sat in front of the TV, hugging her pillow to her chest. Her foot was tied with a piece of cloth where Granny had taken out the splinter with a needle.

"Corrina," called Granny as she chopped onions, "gather up your and Lonnie's clothes."

"Oh, Ma! I hate washing. Can't I watch TV a few more minutes? And my foot hurts."

"Gal, you don't know what washing clothes is. Remember when I had to wash on that old scrub board?"

I was glad I couldn't remember. Granny was proud of her washing machine with a wringer to squeeze out the water from the clothes. She had bought it secondhand from Mitchell's Appliances.

Momma limped on her sore foot all morning. Later she helped me hang a basket of wet sheets on the clothesline to dry in the sun. I held a corner of the heavy sheet to the line while Momma handed a clothespin to me.

Momma giggled as she squeezed open a clothespin. "Don't they look like funny little soldiers doing jumping jacks?"

After we finished, I escaped to the tire swing that hung from the huge oak tree in front of our house. I slipped my skinny legs through the tire, pushed off with my bare feet, and looked up at the moss dangling from the branches. Momma was probably back in the house watching television.

But soon I heard her singing, *"Skip, skip, skip to my Lou. Skip, skip, skip to my Lou. Skip, skip, skip to my Lou. Skip to my Lou, my dar-lin'."*

I saw her skipping shadow on the white sheets. Momma was like the wind blowing gently through the trees as she danced around the sheets, causing them to wave. She must have forgotten all about her sore foot. I wondered how Granny could have one daughter who was so smart and fancy and another daughter who was happy just being plain simple.

As Momma danced and sang, I remembered how we had played dolls together when I was younger, pretending we lived in fairyland. We wore crocheted doilies on our heads for hats, drank magic tea from honeysuckles, and called the dead pine needles gold. Now I felt like I was growing up past her.

I was six when I first realized Momma wasn't the same as other mothers. One time she had played hide-and-seek with my Sunday school class after church. We were all laughing and having a good time, running barefooted through the grass in our best dresses. I remember thinking I was lucky to have a mother who would play games. Then a few minutes later she started crying when she couldn't find us. Later I asked Granny why Momma had cried. Her face went white and she told me to run along and play. I never asked Granny about Momma again. But over the years I learned that Momma was like a child—happy when everything was going fine, upset if something stopped her fun.

❦   ❦   ❦

That afternoon Jesse Wade Thompson walked down our dirt road toward the house with a bat and mitt in his hand. He didn't have to spend any time outside feeding chickens, cutting grass, or working in his daddy's nursery. He only went outside to play.

"Want to hit a few?" he asked, smiling so big his dimples made tiny valleys on his cheeks.

"Nope," I said, trying to ignore the tingling in my right hand—the same feeling I got every time I went up to bat.

"Tiger Ann, I have never seen a day when you didn't want to play baseball. What changed your mind?"

"I'm giving up the game," I said. "Just a silly old game anyway." My stomach rumbled.

"What?" he said. The word came out squeaky like a bicycle wheel that needed oiling. "You can hit the ball farther than anybody in Saitter. Or is that it? Have you lost your golden swing?"

"Of course not."

He swung the bat so clumsily I wanted to yank it from him and show him how to do it right. "That's it, isn't it? Tiger Ann Parker has lost her golden touch."

I knew he was trying to trick me, but my blood

boiled anyway. "Don't be silly," I said. "You know I can outbat you left-handed."

"I'm not so sure about that anymore. Yep, after all, if you could still make the ball fly, you'd prove it right here and now."

I grabbed the bat from him. One last time. I'd get baseball out of my system and Jesse Wade would know it was my choice to leave this dumb game behind. "Where do you want me to aim?"

His dimples appeared again, and he pointed toward the chicken yard in the pasture. "Right out there."

I took my position and spat on the ground.

"Left-handed," he ordered.

"Suit yourself," I said.

Switching the bat to the other hand, I aimed to the right of the henhouse. Jesse Wade took his place in front of me. He spat on the ball and tossed it in the air a few times.

"Jesse Wade, hurry up!"

He looked me square in the eyes and frowned. Leaning back, he pulled back his arm, then threw the ball.

I kept my eye on the ball, slowing the spin down in my mind, seeing each rotation until it came to the place I knew well. The place I called Baseball Heaven. I knew if I swung the bat right then, it would be all glory for me.

Smack!

The ball flew up like it was trying to reach the clouds. Glory! Glory! Baseball Heaven! It went over our pasture gate and landed in our chicken yard.

I folded my arms across my chest, looking at Jesse Wade with raised eyebrows.

He whistled, still staring at the place where the ball landed. Turning to me, he asked, "Now doesn't that make you want to play?"

I swallowed a big lump that had gathered in my throat. "Nope." I turned and ran toward the chicken yard to fetch Jesse Wade's ball.

"Nope?" Jesse Wade hollered. "What do you mean, *nope?*"

"Jesse Wade, a girl has to grow up sometime." Glancing back over my shoulder, I saw Jesse Wade looking at me with his face all scrunched up. I opened the gate and scooped up the ball. "Here, catch."

He caught the ball with his mitt, then he stood there, staring, like he was waiting for me to say this was all a big joke.

"I have to go inside and help Granny with the wash." Underwear and colored clothes were waiting, but the real reason I had to leave was I couldn't stand the sight of that bat—it was calling for me.

🦇   🦇   🦇

Right after supper, Momma and I had plopped on the floor to watch the news when we heard Rudy, our rooster, and the hens clucking away like they'd seen a fox.

Granny hollered, "What in tarnation?"

Daddy grabbed his rifle and we all headed outside.

Rudy and the hens raced beyond the chicken yard, their wings flapping wildly. "Pluck, pluck, pluck, pluck!"

Momma flapped her arms and chased them. "Pluck, pluck, pluck!" she copied.

The chicken yard gate was wide open. My stomach sank. I had left the gate open when I went after Jesse Wade's ball. Daddy dashed inside the henhouse, followed by Granny and Momma. I stood waiting in the dusk, my heart pounding in my ears.

"Where's them baby chicks?" Momma cried, following Daddy and Granny out of the henhouse.

"Possums must have got 'em," Daddy said.

Momma whimpered. I knew she was thinking

about those helpless yellow creatures crying, "Peep, peep!" as possums carried them away. I knew she was thinking about it because that's what I was thinking about too.

Granny looked at me. "Do you know anything about this?"

Daddy stared at the ground as if he were feeling my pain.

My stomach flip-flopped. "Yes, ma'am. I'm afraid I left the gate open this afternoon."

"Then I'm afraid," said Granny, "you'll have to pay me back two dozen chicks."

As we ran around the pasture in the dark, catching Rudy and the hens, I couldn't help thinking this was one more good reason why I would never play baseball again.

four

It was pitch-dark the next morning when Granny woke me up. "Come on, Tiger. Rise and shine."

I could have slugged myself for leaving that chicken yard gate open. Now I had to go with Momma and Granny to the Thompsons' garden and pick purple-hull peas to earn money to replace the baby chicks.

Granny shook my shoulder. "Come on, Tiger. Git up!"

I swung my feet around to the side of the bed and rubbed my eyes. To my surprise, Granny handed me a cup of coffee. "Here—this will get you going."

I sat on the edge of my bed, holding the cup, smelling the strong chicory and letting the steam wet my face. When I was a little kid, Momma and I sometimes played house. Granny would give us cof-fee, filling our cups with more milk than coffee and sweetening it with sugar. I had loved sipping that syrupy drink.

But one sip of this morning's coffee made my eyes spring open and the blood rush through my body. It was one hundred percent black—no cream or sugar. I hated the bitter taste. Granny claimed she couldn't get her day started without it. And Momma liked to sip on a cup when ladies came to visit Granny. She reminded me of a little girl playing grown-up—sitting on the couch with a cup and saucer resting on her lap, nodding back and forth like she understood everything the other ladies said.

I sneaked my cup back into the kitchen and dumped the coffee into the sink.

Granny walked in, wearing overalls and a loose button-up shirt. "Git a move on, gal," she said. She walked over to Momma and Daddy's closed bedroom door. "Corrina, I'm not going to tell you one more time to git on out of bed."

"Ma, I'm sleepy!" Momma whined.

I heard the soft tones of Daddy's voice, but I couldn't make out what he said. Whatever he said must have worked because Momma came out of the room in a second. Her black hair was mussed up around her face, but she was still beautiful.

Granny held out a cup of coffee to Momma. Momma dragged the sugar bowl across the kitchen table and stirred in four tablespoons of sugar, then slurped.

Granny went in her bedroom and returned with one of Granddaddy's long-sleeve shirts. She handed it to me. "Here, Tiger. Better put this on or you'll burn that fair skin to a crisp."

After I returned from feeding Rudy and the hens, Granny grabbed three sunbonnets from the back porch and we headed out the door. I would sure enough die before I ever wore one of those.

"When that sun goes to rising," Granny said, "y'all need to put on a sunbonnet." I was going to die. She might as well have buried me in the ground right then.

Granny must have read my thoughts because she added, "You'll be as freckled as a leopard if you don't."

As the moon faded into the blue morning sky, we rode with Daddy to the Thompsons'. Although Jesse Wade's house stood less than a mile from ours, it remained part of a different world. My great-grandfather built our little house with its tin roof fifty years before. Daddy constantly worked on the house, but no matter how much repairing he did, there was always something else waiting to be fixed—siding to paint, loose floorboards to nail, or wall cracks to fill.

The Thompsons' huge brick home resembled houses I'd seen in magazines. The only other house in Saitter that compared was Abby Lynn Anders's home down the road from ours. Mr. Anders owned the other plant nursery in Saitter. Most of the local men either worked at one of the nurseries or at the Longleaf Sawmill. Even Granny had made plant cuttings at Thompson's Nursery to earn a living after Granddaddy died.

As usual the Anders's cows had gotten out of their pasture again and were blocking us on the road. Daddy honked but they didn't budge, just stayed settled down in front of us, chewing their cuds. Granny jumped out of the truck and waved her arms at them. "Git!" she said. "Git on outta here!"

All the cows except Miss Astor slowly moseyed over to the side of the road. That was the reason we called her Miss Astor. She thought she was better than the other cows.

"Git on, I said," Granny hollered. But Miss Astor just stared back at Granny with her big brown eyes. Granny placed her hands on her hips and peered over her glasses at Miss Astor. They were having a stare down. I jumped out of the back of the truck to help

Granny as a little red-faced calf peeked from behind Miss Astor's rear end.

"Well, looky here," said Granny. "Miss Astor is a momma."

"I can go around them," Daddy said. We got back in the truck and headed over to the Thompsons'.

When we arrived, Daddy started toward the nursery on the other side of the Thompsons' manicured lawn. Rows and rows of potted azaleas, junipers, and other green plants spread to a tall-pined horizon. Milton Lambert and Shorty Calhoun were stacking gallon cans near the hothouse.

Mr. Thompson rode up to us on his tractor. He turned the key and the growling engine stopped. The world seemed so quiet except for the mockingbird calling out.

"Morning, folks," he said, removing his hat. The hat rim had made a red mark around his bald head.

"Morning," we called back.

Mr. Thompson looked toward the nursery, where Daddy was grabbing a hose. "Tiger, do you realize your daddy has never missed a day on the job since he was fifteen years old? He's my hardest worker. He always gives me more than an honest day's work. Wish I had ten men like him."

I felt like the sun had sent a beam straight down from the sky to light me up.

"Miz Jewel," he said, "have I shown you a picture of my Louisiana Lady camellia?"

"Don't believe I've ever heard of a Louisiana Lady," said Granny.

Mr. Thompson removed a photograph from his pocket. "That's because she's my creation. Eight years in the making. Ain't she pretty?"

Granny held the picture up close and peered over her glasses. "Whooo-wee!"

Mr. Thompson grinned, looking as proud as a new poppa. "Yep, eight years fussing over her until she made the prettiest blooms. Heck, I had to court her more than I did Arlette."

Granny showed the picture to Momma and me. The flower was full like an open rose. A dark pink crowned the edges of the pale pink petals.

Momma leaned in so close her nose touched the picture. "Whooo-wee! She sure is pretty."

"Yes, sir," I said.

Mr. Thompson placed his hat back on and rested his elbow on his knee. "Got a man in Dallas interested in my camellias. I'm gonna see him in a couple of weeks. Said my camellias could make a nice little sum of money. Their blooms don't crumble easy like so many of the others."

Granny handed back the picture to Mr. Thompson. "Are they early or late bloomers?" she asked.

Mr. Thompson leaned over. "Early. They start in October and bloom through Christmas."

"I declare," Granny said.

"I declare," Momma repeated.

"Miz Jewel," he said, "you make sure you pick a mess of peas for your family before you leave, ya hear?"

"I appreciate that, Woodrow, since my peas didn't make it this year like last. That darn stinkbug."

"You need to spray tobacco on them."

"Is that a fact? Thank you, Woodrow. I'll try that."

Mr. Thompson started up the tractor and hollered, "It's gonna be a scorcher today." He rode off toward the nursery, leaving behind tracks in the moist grass.

Granny tied Momma's bonnet under her chin. Momma smiled real proud like Granny had placed a crown on her head. "I bet I look like you, Ma. Don't I? I bet I look *just* like you."

The corner of Granny's lips curled into a small smile. "God help you if you do, child. Tiger, better put yours on."

I tied the miserable red calico bonnet under my chin, grabbed a bucket, and followed Granny and Momma to the garden to start our chore. Momma started picking everything on the vine including the green peas and the dried-up ones.

Granny took the bucket from her and shook it upside down. Then she handed the bucket back to Momma. "Only the purple ones, Corrina."

Every time we filled a bucket, we dumped the peas into a bushel basket at the end of the row. At first it seemed like a game to see how fast I could fill the bucket, but I soon tired of snapping peas from the vine and hearing them land with a *tink, tink* against the metal.

We must have been a sight to see, the three of us standing between rows of pink-eyed purple hulls—a big old lady in overalls, a pretty childlike woman, and a skinny redhead with bony knees—all with sun-bonnets plopped on our heads. I would die if Abby Lynn or Jesse Wade saw me like this.

A few hours later Jesse Wade came out of his house and sat on the wicker porch swing, looking in our direction. He pretended to read something— probably a Superman comic book, but I saw him peek at us over the pages.

Later he disappeared, then returned with a flow-
ered dishcloth tied around his head and a basket in
his hand. He pranced around the porch, bending
down like he was picking something to put in his
basket. He looked like he was playing a game we
played in the church nursery when we were younger.
But then I realized exactly what he was doing. The
monkey. No matter what I looked like, I knew I
didn't look that silly. Despite myself, I laughed.

Granny's voice brought me back to my chore and
the reason I was here. "Tiger, what are you doing?"
She stood straight, rubbing the small of her back.

Of course, by then Jesse Wade had sat down inno-
cently and pretended to read again.

"You better get back to work," Granny said. "You
should be working harder than anyone. Remember?
You have twenty-four chickens to pay back."

"Yes, ma'am."

When she bent down again to pick the peas, I
stuck out my tongue at Jesse Wade, and he did the
same back to me. Even though Jesse Wade brightened my boring job for a moment, I couldn't help
but think about how he was the reason I was out here
working my fingers to the bone and sweating under
the sun.

At that moment I decided Jesse Wade was spoiled rotten. He used nice manners, saying, "Yes, ma'am," and "No, sir," but he'd never done a lick of work in his life. And here his daddy had this fine nursery. Granny said Mrs. Thompson had spoiled Jesse Wade because he had been such a sickly baby. But the way I figured it, if Jesse Wade could hit a baseball and run bases he should be able to do a few chores.

At noon we broke for lunch. As we took our pails to the screen porch, Mrs. Thompson brought out iced tea and lemonade on a tray for us. She looked so crisp and clean in her white blouse and pink pedal pushers. I wished I had a pair of pedal pushers that cuffed at the calves like hers instead of my baggy shorts.

I looked at Momma's loose housedress and silly sunbonnet. Suddenly she dropped her lunch pail and dashed toward a corner, grabbing something.

"I got it!" Momma held up a chameleon. "I got a lizard!" She shoved the gaping green creature under Mrs. Thompson's nose.

Mrs. Thompson jumped back. "You sure did, Corrina. You're even faster than Jesse Wade."

"Put it down," said Granny.

Momma pouted but set the chameleon free. She picked up her lunch pail and sat on the porch swing.

Mrs. Thompson placed the tray on a small table between two aluminum chairs. "Surely y'all aren't going to spend too much more time doing this, are you?"

"I reckon we'll see sunset here," Granny said, settling her behind on one of the aluminum chairs.

Mrs. Thompson sat in the other chair and poured a glass of tea for Granny and lemonade for Momma, Jesse Wade, and me. "Miz Jewel, now you watch yourself," Mrs. Thompson said. "Don't work too hard."

"Oh, this is nothing like the hard work I've seen in my seventy-two years."

Here she goes, I thought. Talking about the good ole days. I could practically recite her speech myself.

"In the good old days," Granny said, "we didn't know what life was like if we didn't go to bed with aching bones and throbbing muscles."

"You don't say?" said Mrs. Thompson. I thought it was real nice how Mrs. Thompson could act so interested in someone who was saying the most uninteresting things.

Momma took a sip of lemonade and squinted. "Can I have some sugar, Miz Thompson? This lemonade is as sour as Ma's pickles."

"Corrina!" Granny snapped, tea spraying out of her mouth.

"That's quite all right, Miz Jewel. Corrina, you're right, *ma chère*! Woodrow likes his lemonade kind of sour, so I always serve it with sugar on the side. I just forgot to bring it out today. Thanks for reminding me." She went into the house and returned with a sugar bowl.

While Momma scooped several spoons of sugar into her glass, Jesse Wade asked me, "Want to go sit over there under the tree?"

"Sure," I said, yanking off that goofy bonnet.

"Don't take off too far, Tiger," Granny hollered. "We didn't come to play." My aching bones and throbbing muscles knew that for sure. We ate our sandwiches in a hurry and lay under the shade of the oak tree while we studied clouds floating by. "That one's a carriage with three horses," I said, pointing to the sky.

"Where?" Jesse Wade asked.

"There, see." We sometimes played this game when we were bored. It was funny how whatever was heavy on our minds floated right up from our heads to the sky and made a picture. Thinking about those rows and rows of purple hulls waiting to be picked made me desperately wish for a horse-pulled carriage to carry me away—maybe to visit Aunt Dorie Kay in Baton Rouge.

Jesse Wade propped up on his elbows. "Did you hear about Abby Lynn's new swimming pool?"

"Nope," I said, trying not to act like that was the most exciting news I had heard all summer. I had never seen a real swimming pool.

Before long, Granny called me back, and I dragged my feet to the garden. Jesse Wade caught up with me. "Don't forget this, Tiger." He held out that stupid bonnet, grinning at me with his dimples showing. "You might freckle up like a strawberry. In fact, I see a big freckle right there." He touched the tip of my nose.

I snatched the bonnet from his hand and headed out to the garden.

By midafternoon my legs throbbed and my back ached something fierce. Why was it that when I played baseball or went swimming in the creek, the sun slipped down as fast as butter melts on toast, but today it inched down as slow as a caterpillar crawls across Texas? Granny was a slave driver when it came to chores. It was as if she had to prove to everyone that she was a hard worker even though she was an old lady.

By three o'clock Momma plopped down on the ground. "I can't do it no more! I'm tired and I hurt." We had already picked four bushels of peas.

"Where do you hurt?" Granny asked.

"Everywhere!"

"Get up, Corrina. You don't see Tiger and me stopping, do you?"

But a few moments later when I was staring at the Thompsons' house, wondering where Jesse Wade had gone to in his privileged life, Granny said, "Tiger, stop your daydreaming. Gracious, I have one daydreamer and one whiner."

At five o'clock Daddy was off work, and he joined us in the garden until the sun dropped into a pink-and-lavender horizon. I never thought I'd welcome the end of the day like I did this one.

"Okay," Granny finally said, "let's call it a day."

"Amen!" hollered Momma.

"Amen," I whispered under my breath.

five

Momma, Jesse Wade, and I floated on inner tubes at Saitter Creek with our legs dangling over the rubber and our feet dipping in the cold water. It was mid-June, and the day was hotter than the Fourth of July. My hand shaded my eyes from the sun as I watched clouds dance around the tips of trees towering above us, and listened to the grasshoppers chirping loudly in the tall grass.

"Watch this," Momma said in her high voice.

To my horror, she plopped into the creek and ducked her head under the water.

"No, Momma!" I yelled. Granny had told us not to get our hair wet since we were going to the book-mobile today. I waited a second, but Momma didn't bounce back up. The air left my lungs like someone had slapped it out of me. I jumped into the water, reaching, trying to feel for one of Momma's arms or legs. Anything. But I touched nothing. Now I was afraid for more than Granny's scolding.

"Jesse Wade, do something quick!" I screamed, splashing water on him and waking him from his doze.

He shook his head and opened his eyes. "What?"

"It's my momma! She's gone under the water."

"She always comes back up."

"Well, she hasn't come up yet! Help me!"

He dove into the creek and swam under the water toward the other end. Momma's empty inner tube floated lazily on the surface. I kept my arms stretched out, grabbing with my hands, but I only captured creek water. My heart pounded so fast, I thought it would leap from my chest.

Just as Jesse Wade's head bobbed above the surface and I had decided to dunk mine under, I heard Momma's giggle behind me.

"Here I am! Here I am!" she chanted, holding on to her inner tube. Her wet stringy hair didn't hide her beauty. Her cheeks looked kissed by the sun, and her eyes sparkled like the sunbeams dancing on the water. When she finally stopped laughing, she said, "Bet you can't do that!"

I sighed with relief. "Oh, Momma, Granny's gonna skin us alive." But I was so thankful to see her breathing, I hugged her.

She hugged me back, then said, "Want to see what old Clem does when he's had a swim?" Clem was Jesse Wade's hound dog.

Before I could answer, she shook her head over and over, her wet locks spitting water at me.

"Hey, quit it, Momma!"

She giggled and Jesse Wade laughed. Then she stopped and stared at something past us.

"Hi, Ma," Momma said.

Jesse Wade rolled off his inner tube. "Hi, Miz Jewel."

I whipped around. Granny stood on the creek bank, frowning, with two towels in her hands.

Momma kept grinning. "Look, Ma. You want to see what old Clem does after a swim?" She repeated her shaking act, but this time no one laughed.

"Come here, Corrina," Granny said. "Let's get you dried off. You can't go to the bookmobile with wet hair." She looked at me. "Believe I told you that earlier."

Momma stepped forward and Granny tossed a towel to me. She threw the other over Momma's head, then rubbed it viciously.

"Ow, Ma!" Momma cried. "That hurts."

Granny continued rubbing. "Maybe you'll remember that next time I tell you not to wet your hair. Now git on to the house and git dressed."

Momma headed home singing, *"How much is that doggy in the window?"* She disappeared behind the brush, but we could still hear her. *"Ruff, ruff!"*

"I'm sorry, Granny," I said. "She went under before I could do anything."

Granny's face softened into a smile. Not a big smile because that wasn't her way, but a smile just the same. "Don't fret," she said. "Expect you better get back and change too. At least you both won't be going with dripping hair. Jesse Wade, you tell your momma hello for me. And tell your daddy those purple hulls were mighty good." She turned and walked away.

"Yes, ma'am. I sure will, ma'am." Jesse Wade looked as relieved as I felt.

A half hour later Momma and I walked to the bookmobile parked outside the Saitter Creek School gym. As we walked, we took turns kicking a rock, a game we often played to make the two miles go quicker.

Once inside the bookmobile, I checked out *Little Women* for the second time as Momma looked through

the picture books. Hannah stood in the back, brows-
ing at *Jane Eyre*. She wore a new cast on her arm. A
few months ago she had claimed her ribs had broken
from a fall, but I wondered if it was true what everybody said about her daddy beating her.

When she saw me staring at her, she frowned.
"That's a good book," I said. "I read it last summer."
She put it back on the shelf and selected another. I
quickly turned my head and looked out the window.
Abby Lynn, Dolly, Annette, and Jackie were going
inside the gym.

I glanced back at Momma. She kept looking over
each book like other mothers select the best pork
chops. She held a book in each hand, her eyes looking from the right to the left. Over and over again.
She would be there until the bookmobile had to
drive away.

I sneaked outside and slipped into the gym. Some
of the boys, including Jesse Wade, played basketball
while Abby Lynn and the other girls stood near the
bleachers. They formed a circle, leaving me on the
outside as Abby Lynn flipped through a Sears Roebuck catalog. They all wore matching saddle oxfords
and barrettes in their bobbed hair. I wondered what I
might look like with saddle oxfords on my feet and a
bobbed hairdo.

Abby Lynn pointed to something in the catalog pages. "I like this swimming suit with the ruffle."

"Ooh, yes," said the other girls together.

Abby Lynn closed the catalog. "My daddy says when the swimming pool is finished, I can have a swimming party. I'm going to invite everybody I know."

She looked at me when she said that. My heart pounded.

Then I heard, "Tiger! Tiger!"

Momma was calling me. Her loud sobs rose above the murmurs in the crowded gym.

People stopped talking and stared across the room at Momma. Even Jesse Wade stopped dribbling. Momma stood with her feet wide apart holding her opened purse in one hand and a picture book in the other. Her hair was still damp from the swim and red lipstick smeared past the edges of her mouth.

The girls giggled. My face burned like a kerosene lamp. I wished I could slither into a crack in the wall.

"Tiger, your momma is looking for you." Abby Lynn's blond curls bounced to the rhythm of each word she spoke.

Dolly closed her lips and frowned, covering the big gap between her two front teeth. "Why, Tiger Parker, did you go off and leave your momma by herself? Shame on you!" The other girls snickered.

My body froze as I looked at the scratched wood floor. I should have waved my arm high and said, "Here, Momma. Here I am." Instead I kept still and wished I could be invisible. Could this really be happening? Maybe it was a dream.

But it was no dream.

Momma's outburst probably ruined any chance for an invitation to that swimming party. People divided as if Momma were Moses parting the Red Sea. Her black patent leather purse gaped open and the handle rested in the crook of her arm. She looked around, scoping out the gym. My heart pounded like a drum. Finally her eyes met mine and she raced toward me, grabbed me, and wrapped her sweaty arms around my waist. Her cheek pressed against mine.

"Here you are, Tiger!"

Abby Lynn whispered in Dolly's ear, and the girls giggled.

Momma squeezed me. Her hair covered my face. "I thought I lost you, and I didn't know where lost and found was."

Abby Lynn smothered her laughter, covering her mouth with her hand. I was doomed. But I couldn't blame Momma for saying it. Once when I was four, I got lost shopping with her in Penney's. Then Granny taught us to go to the lost-and-found department if it happened again.

Momma had cried then, too. "Tiger, please don't play hide-and-seek. I don't like that game."

The girls backed away from us, leaving Momma and me in our own little circle. Every person in the gym stared at us as if we were performing a play. I noticed Jesse Wade from across the room. When my gaze reached his, he looked down at the floor. Then he lifted his head and smiled at me.

"Come on, Momma. Let's go home." I glanced at the girls quickly on the way out.

We left the gym to walk back home. Minnie and Abner, whose father, Otis, worked with Daddy at the nursery, strolled past the school yard and waved to us. Minnie wore her hair in a dozen braids. Each one had a red ribbon tied around the end. She and Abner were probably going to the colored school to meet the bookmobile there.

Momma held her book, *The Little Engine That Could,* in one hand and swung her purse with the other as she kicked a rock with the scuffed toe of her Sunday shoe. "Your turn."

"No thanks," I grumbled.

"What's wrong?" she asked.

"I don't feel like it."

"But you kicked rocks when we walked to school. Why don't you want to play now?"

"Because I don't feel like it!" I shouted.

Momma didn't have the sense to know why I was angry. My anger surprised her as well as me. I never yelled at Momma.

Her face wrinkled up like one of the toddlers in our church nursery. "You're mad at me. Why are you mad at me?"

I didn't speak because I didn't know what to say. I felt shameful and odd, as though the thoughts running through my head belonged to someone else. I wished I hadn't gone inside the gym. I wished I hadn't seen Abby Lynn and the other girls. But most of all, for the first time I wished Momma wasn't my momma.

She cried and tried to touch my arm but I shrugged away. "You are mad at me. What did I do?"

I hunched my shoulders. "Momma, why did you have to go hugging on me at the gym?"

She stopped walking and gasped. Her hand flew to her mouth as her huge brown eyes grew larger. "Did I squeeze you too tight?"

"Oh, forget it." I started to walk again.

Momma followed, her head hung low like she'd been punished. Guilt swallowed me whole. How could I ever cheer her up? I kicked a rock. "Your turn, Momma."

She giggled, shaking off her sad mood like old Clem shaking off a swim.

"Hold these," she said, handing her book and purse to me. She spotted the stone ahead of her and backed up. Puffing out her cheeks, she pushed off with one foot and ran a few steps. Her foot kicked the stone so hard, it flew toward the sky until it crashed into our mailbox. She brushed her hands together and smiled. "Bet you can't do that."

"No, Momma. I bet I can't." I followed Momma up the winding path to our home. The midday sun peeked between towering pine trees and its heat beat down on my body. I thought how nice it might feel to be invited to Abby Lynn's swimming party and go swimming in a real swimming pool.

six

Life started to change all around me after that day at the gym. Sometimes I looked at Momma and Daddy and my face heated up thinking about what they might do next to embarrass me.

Other times I thought about some of my best memories with them and I felt ashamed. Like the time when I was nine and we went to the Louisiana State Fair in Shreveport. Granny sat on a bench while Daddy, Momma, and I rode the Ferris wheel.

Each time our cart left the ground, Daddy said, "Here we go—up, up, up!"

On the ride down, Momma and I squealed the whole way. We rode that Ferris wheel sixteen times. We would have rode seventeen times, but I got sick and threw up.

One thing that bothered me about Momma was

her television watching. Seemed like she stayed glued to that TV from the day I turned it on. She hurried through her chores, then plopped onto her bed pillow on the floor two feet from the set and watched everything from *Howdy Doody* to *The Guiding Light*.

She watched late into the night until they played the national anthem before ending the day's broadcast. As soon as the music started, Momma stood at attention, placed her hand over her heart, and sang out in a flat tone, *"Ohhh, say can you see . . ."*

Daddy soon tired of the television and, like Granny, called it the "noise box." He was happiest working with his hands and never sat down much. "Don't see much point sitting and watching other people live their lives," he'd say. When his day ended at the nursery, he worked in Granny's garden.

Before Aunt Dorie Kay bought the television, Momma watched for Daddy every day, the same way she waited for me to come home from school. From the road, her face looked like a doll's perched in the window between the parted calico curtains. By the time Daddy reached the top porch step, she flung open the door, dashed up to him, and threw her arms around his skinny body. Then she pressed her puckered lips on his. They held each other for the longest time. Sometimes the way Momma and Daddy ogled each other made me blush. I couldn't tell you why. I only know Momma acted as if Daddy was handsome as Marlon Brando, and Lord knows he wasn't.

A couple of days after we went to the bookmobile, Momma didn't greet Daddy at the door. He marched back down the porch steps again and stomped back up in his heavy boots. *Tromp. Tromp. Tromp.* The screen door squeaked and he slowly opened the front door, then peeked into the room. His smile disappeared when he discovered her sitting cross-legged in front of the evening news with Edward R. Murrow.

He cleared his throat. "Hello, Corrina. How was your day?"

She glanced his way, then blew him a kiss. She had seen an actress do that on TV.

He ran his fingers through his hair and raised his voice, competing with Mr. Murrow's hypnotic tone. "I said, *'How was your day?'* "

She barely turned her chin. "The Reds are shaking hands with the Americans." Momma had no idea a Red was a communist. She just heard someone say it on television.

Daddy slammed the back door, causing Granny's

rising bread loaves to flatten. Granny sighed and shook her head.

The next morning I told Momma Granny wanted her to help me get the laundry off the clothesline before a summer storm settled in. She stretched her arms out in front of her, spun in a circle, and imitated Jackie Gleason from *The Honeymooners* show.

"To the moon, Alice. To the moon," she said.

I couldn't have a conversation with her anymore without her saying something she had heard on television.

Later in the afternoon Momma settled in front of the television again. Her voice chirped in glee. *"It's Howdy Doody time. . . ."*

How many other mothers watched a stupid puppet show? Abby Lynn and the other girls would laugh if they caught sight of Momma on her pillow, engrossed in a kiddie program.

Thank goodness for Granny. Standing beside her in the warm kitchen, I chopped celery as she added spices to the chicken gumbo on the stove. A feed sack apron surrounded her waist.

"Smells good, Granny."

"Thank you, sugar. I ordered some more chicks today."

"You did?"

"Mmm-hmm. Should be here by next week some-time. Why don't you watch television with your momma? You've helped me plenty and dinner will be ready soon enough."

I glanced at Momma watching the goofy, freckled puppet and his sidekick, Buffalo Bob. Grabbing a damp rag, I wiped the Formica table. "That's okay. I don't like that dumb show. Don't know why anyone would like it. Anyone with sense wouldn't."

Granny arched an eyebrow. "You mean anyone but your momma?"

I rubbed the cloth viciously over an old scratch. "I didn't say that." I felt the shame of speaking my mind, but Granny was the only person I could talk to. Maybe she could shed light on my feelings for Momma and Daddy.

Drying her hands on the apron, she asked, "Some-body say something about your momma, Tiger?"

"Not exactly."

"Not exactly usually means yes or no. Which is it?"

While I told her about what happened at the gym, Momma giggled at the show. No need to worry about her overhearing me. A hurricane wouldn't faze her.

Granny listened patiently, leaning over the kitchen counter. When I finished my story, she said, "People are afraid of what's different. That don't mean different is bad. Just means different is different."

I knew Granny was right, but words couldn't help my problem. They couldn't give Momma and Daddy smarter brains or get me invited to Abby Lynn's swimming party.

I didn't tell Granny I wished Momma wasn't different. Maybe she suspected already, because as I left the kitchen, she squeezed in the last word.

"Perhaps those girls don't deserve your friendship. Besides, you have Jesse Wade."

My class had eleven students and those girls were the only ones in my class. How could I survive seventh grade with Jesse Wade Thompson as my only friend?

🐚　　🐚　　🐚

That week Daddy stomped around the house so hard it shook. He slammed doors until two jars of fig preserves fell from a shelf and broke. Then Granny made a new rule—only two hours of television a day.

Momma pleaded. When that didn't work, she pouted. But Granny didn't budge or back down.

Pretty soon our routine returned to what it had

been before the "noise box" came into our lives. Momma slowed her pace and took more time with her chores. Daddy got his hugs and kisses. But I still didn't get invited to Abby Lynn's swimming party.

Maybe Abby Lynn had tried to call. Since we shared a phone line with four other families, it might have been busy. Especially since Miz Eula was one of those other people.

Then one night as I lay on my back in the cool grass watching fireflies dance against an ebony sky, a thought occurred to me. Abby Lynn was a fancy person. She probably would do everything real proper. Maybe she had sent paper invitations through the mail. There might be one waiting in our mailbox that very minute. But the evening was too dark to walk the half mile to see if my hunch was right. I would have to wait until the next day.

seven

In the morning I scurried in bare feet down the winding path through the grass to the mailbox. I did that every day for a whole week. Even Brando knew my routine. Like a set clock, he waited for me at the bottom of the porch steps and tagged behind me. And each day I met disappointment as I shuffled through the envelopes.

I grew so tired of our mailman Horace Tanner's whiskered face. I tried to time it so that I arrived at the mailbox after Horace, but each day I managed to get there just as his old blue Chevy drove up.

He had a new set of nosy questions for me every day. Wednesday he asked, "You expecting big money from some contest, Tiger Parker?"

On Thursday it was, "Are you waiting for a love letter from an old beau?" He'd grin, revealing coffee-stained teeth with black spaces between them.

Six days after Abby Lynn announced she was having a swimming party, Horace rolled down his window and handed our mail to me with a rubber band around it. "Did somebody die and leave you insurance money?"

I wondered what was happening to the U.S. Postal Service to hire greasy old Horace. Until last year Mr. Henry Odom delivered our mail. He was kind and respectable.

After a week of bills and one letter from Aunt Dorie Kay, I decided to stop thinking about the silly invitation. For all I knew, Abby Lynn's party had come and gone. The sun's heat caused beads of sweat to slither down my temples and neck. Who needed a swimming pool? Saitter Creek had been my favorite swimming hole ever since I could remember.

As I changed into my baggy swimming suit, I wondered if Abby Lynn had ordered that red one with a ruffle from the Sears Roebuck catalog. Abby Lynn's and the other girls' developing figures probably filled their suits across the top and bottom. Most of them already wore a bra.

Granny said, "Trees bud out at different times in the spring." But my blossoming was taking a few seasons. Seemed like the things I didn't want to change did, and the things I did, didn't.

With a towel draped over my shoulder, I rolled an inner tube down the road to Jesse Wade's house. When I arrived at the Thompsons' home, I left my tube on the ground and ran up the porch steps. While I waited for someone to answer the door, I turned and looked toward the nursery. Otis was shoveling dirt into a wheelbarrow near a hothouse and Daddy was wrapping plant root balls with burlap.

The door opened and a startled look crossed Mrs. Thompson's face. "Tiger, Jesse Wade already left for the swimming party about an hour ago. Were the two of you supposed to attend together? Goodness, that child is getting so forgetful."

My face flushed and I hunched my shoulders. "Swimming party?" I swallowed and tried to sound natural. "Oh, you mean he's already left for Abby Lynn's house?"

"Yes. I'm sorry, he sure has. Do you need a ride, *ma chère?*"

My voice squeaked out of me in a high pitch I hardly recognized. "No, ma'am. I can walk. . . . I'll see him later." I turned around quickly to avoid her eyes meeting mine.

As I dashed down the steps and grabbed my tube, she called after me, "You can still make the party. Have fun, Tiger."

I ran down the path, awkwardly dragging the chubby tube behind me. When I reached the dirt road, I didn't stop. How could Jesse Wade go to Abby Lynn's party without me?

My vision blurred, and when a car drove by, I didn't wave like I usually did. I just kept running to the pace of my beating heart. Dust from the red dirt stirred, flying into my eyes. I stopped because I couldn't see where I was going. I rubbed my eyes with my towel and cried, "I hate you, Abby Lynn Anders. I hate you."

A moment later I heard the car stop down the road a ways and someone slammed the door. As I spun around, the car turned, continuing toward the Thompson house, while a boy walked slowly toward me. It was Jesse Wade. He wore an open plaid shirt and wet swim trunks. He approached me with a towel slung over his shoulder and a shy smile on his face.

I walked away as quickly as I could, dragging my stupid inner tube.

His footsteps quickened behind me. "Wait, Tiger Ann."

Catching up to my slowed pace, he reached out and grabbed my arm. "I'm sorry, Tiger Ann. I know."

I wiggled my arm from his grasp. "You know

what?" He was my best friend and he had betrayed me.

He looked down at his feet and kicked some dirt. His voice grew soft. "I know Abby Lynn didn't invite you."

I stayed quiet. The awful feeling inside me kept growing, taking up space in my stomach and pressing against my chest.

"I didn't know when I went to the party," he explained. "In fact, I tried to call this morning, but no one answered. So I reckoned you had already left."

Momma and that stupid TV. "How did you find out I wasn't invited?"

"When I didn't see you anywhere, I asked Abby Lynn where you were. After she told me you weren't invited, I asked Daddy to take me home. He was visiting with Mr. Anders." He turned his head away from my accusing eyes.

"Great! Now everyone knows I wasn't invited." I didn't want to cry in front of him, but tears came and my nose began to leak. I cleaned my face with the towel.

Jesse Wade inched toward me. His arms embraced me for the first time since I'd known him and our foreheads touched.

"It's not fair. I didn't do anything to them."

I felt safe in his arms and my shaking body soon calmed. But then his lips aimed toward mine. I turned my head and the kiss landed on my cheek. For a slight moment I thought he was being brotherly, but he tried once more. This time he held my chin until his lips met mine. My stomach rumbled. This wasn't Marlon Brando kissing me. This was my best buddy. My head spun and I felt dizzy. I thrust my hands against his chest and backed away. Then, abandoning my inner tube, I turned and ran all the way home.

eight

When I reached home, I wiped my face with my towel again before going inside. The sight of Miz Eula's rusty car parked in our driveway made me forget about the kiss for a moment.

Momma and Granny were busy listening to Miz Eula at the kitchen table. Fabric scraps puddled the floor and Granny's black Singer sewing machine stood erect in its cabinet. A Simplicity pattern of a girl's plain dress lay on the table. Usually I would have asked a million questions about the dresses, but Miz Eula's tales paled the excitement of my new school wardrobe.

Miz Eula raised her pointy chin and flapped her mouth at high speed. Straight pins stuck out between Granny's tight lips as she tried to appear uninterested in Miz Eula's latest news. Granny often said, "Gossip is for idle ears and hands." But with her ear tilted toward Miz Eula, she seemed interested just the same.

Momma didn't bother to pretend that she wasn't interested. She leaned forward with her idle hands on the table and idle ears wide open. "Hannah?" asked Momma.

"What about Hannah?" I asked, trying to erase the picture in my mind of Jesse Wade kissing me.

Miz Eula smirked. "Hello, Tiger. Well, what I was telling your momma and granny is Hannah up and married J.T. Webster night before last."

"What? Mr. Webster is an old man."

Miz Eula chuckled loudly. "Well, it depends on what you think old is." She leaned over, patted Granny's hand, and winked at her. But Granny kept pinning the sleeve to the armhole of a blue dress. Miz Eula glanced back at me. "Some of us think thirty-nine is pretty young. But he *is* too old for that child."

My mind tried to picture fourteen-year-old Hannah with Mr. Webster, but I couldn't see it. Mr. Webster's wife died last winter and left him with three children. The oldest was my age and the youngest wore diapers. I thought about Mr. Webster kissing Hannah the way Jesse Wade kissed me moments before. My stomach turned and I sank to the cool linoleum.

Lifting an eyebrow, Granny removed the last pin and said, "Tiger, you might want to go to the bedroom and take your clothes off for a fitting." She probably meant, "Tiger, you've heard enough."

Miz Eula didn't get the hint. She leaned closer, pointing her chin at me. "You knew her daddy beat her?"

Granny released the sleeve, dropping it to the table. "Eula!"

Miz Eula's body twisted toward Granny. "Well, everyone knows it, Jewel. Anyway, the girl had enough. She and J.T. eloped night before last. Snatched her from under her daddy's drunk nose." She twisted her torso toward me. "Passed out on the couch is what I heard. But what else is new? When her daddy got word of the marriage, he headed straight over to J.T.'s house with a rifle. Started hollering and carrying on. He said Hannah was good for a few more years of chores at home and J.T. might as well have robbed him because a young gal like her was worth more money than he had in the bank. Didn't know he had any money in the bank. Did you, Jewel?"

Granny ignored Miz Eula's question. Pins were sticking out of her mouth again.

I wondered if Hannah would go to school anymore. How could she be a child one minute and someone's wife another? That picture of Jesse Wade and me flashed in my mind again, refusing to leave.

While Miz Eula gabbed, Momma's cheek rested on her hand as she hung on every word.

Miz Eula sipped a cup of coffee and continued, "Word has it J.T. gave him his truck to let her stay. Can you imagine? Swapped his daughter for a '42 pickup? Anyway, that's all I know. Sure hope the child knows how to . . ."

"Eula!" Granny shouted as the pins fell out of her mouth.

"Cook," Miz Eula finished. She stood, lifting her handbag. "Well, I expect I better be leaving. Got to get my man fed."

After Miz Eula left, Granny plopped in front of the sewing machine. It clanked as she guided fabric under the needle.

Momma rarely used the machine because she liked handwork best. Granny never bragged much, but she praised Momma's dainty stitches. "Only a born seamstress can sew such fine stitches, Corrina."

Whenever Granny said that, Momma smiled real big and glanced around as if to see who heard the compliment.

One of Granny's biggest virtues was her honesty. I learned early in life not to ask a question unless I was prepared for the truth. Once I asked her if I was pretty.

"No, Tiger. You're not. But you're smart and that's more important."

Her words stung. I remembered thinking I'd rather be pretty. Every time I caught a glimpse of Abby Lynn's flaxen curls, my wish to be pretty grew stronger.

The pinned hemline hit above my thin calves. I examined myself in the mirror, wishing I could close my eyes and turn this little-girl-style dress into a full skirt with a record or a poodle on it. Jesse Wade's face slipped into my thoughts. My face grew hot. How was I ever going to get that stupid kiss out of my mind?

I modeled one of the dresses for Momma and Granny. The unhemmed dress was a gray-blue, like a Louisiana sky after a hard rain. A white collar trimmed the neckline. I tried to stand without fidgeting as Momma pinned up the hem.

Momma stepped back and admired me. "That blue sure looks pretty on you, Tiger." Funny thing was, Momma always told me I was pretty and I think she really believed it.

Granny cut three dresses of different colors from the same pattern. The cream and yellow pieces lay in a pile waiting to be sewn. I'd be teased for wearing yellow. "Red and yella kill a fella," the kids would say. The rhyme reminded folks how to identify poisonous snakes, but some people never passed up a chance to tease a plain, redheaded girl.

After Momma put the fabric away, she settled on her pillow and watched TV. Granny tied an apron around her thick waist from the front, then twisted the knot to the back. "Tiger, it's time you learned to make chicken and dumplings."

"But Granny, you always said chicken and dumplings was your one secret recipe."

Granny slid the flour canister off a shelf. "Oh, pshaw, gal. I just didn't have the patience to show you before. But it's time now."

Time for what? I wondered. Hannah popped into my head. "Granny, are you trying to get me ready for marrying?"

Granny laughed. She kept laughing until her eyes

filled with tears. Her black bun shook on top of her head as she dropped the flour scoop, causing a white cloud. "Lord, child, what made you say that?"

I felt my face blush, feeling foolish over my question. "I don't know. Maybe Hannah marrying old Mr. Webster."

Granny wiped tears from her plump cheeks. "Hannah is not you. Tiger, you're a smart gal when it comes to those books, but you've got a lot of learning to do when it comes to life."

I tucked the dish towel edge between the waistband of my blue jeans and shirt as I watched Granny throw her ingredients together. She never used a measuring cup or spoon. She always knew what dumplings needed—a little more water, milk, or flour. She just knew. Her hands seemed to know the recipe by heart.

I compared our hands. My fingers were long and thin while Granny's fingers were short and stubby. I could barely see the veins in my hands. Granny's veins were raised and blue like roads on a map. I loved her hands. They had scratched my back on sleepless nights. They had wiped my tears. And now they were showing me how to make her famous dumplings.

Granny dusted the wooden rolling pin with flour. "The secret is don't play with the dough too much. Makes 'em tough. And for heaven's sake, roll 'em out thin. Can't stand thick dumplings."

I turned the floured rolling pin over the dough under her watchful eye. As she hummed to a song on the radio, I felt relieved that I had Granny.

After we ate supper and washed dishes, we settled on the screened porch. Crickets chirped, and smells of chicken and dumplings still lingered among us. Momma brushed my hair gently as I read *Little Women* aloud. Granny and Daddy sat on the porch swing and shelled butter beans from her garden.

When I finished the chapter, Granny said, "I need to finish picking a mess of butter beans tomorrow. They'll go bad if I don't."

🐝　　🐝　　🐝

Lying in my bed that night, I should have thanked the good Lord for what I did have. I felt sorry for Hannah. She didn't have a family that loved her like mine. Even if Momma and Daddy were slow, Granny had enough brains for all of us. I wished Abby Lynn's dumb swimming party didn't mean so much, but it did.

Brushing my fingers across my lips, I thought about the afternoon. I reckon I always knew I would have a first kiss, but I never in a million years thought Jesse Wade would be the one to deliver it.

Suddenly light slipped under my doorway, coming from Granny's room across the hall. I got up and knocked softly on her door.

"Come in," she called out.

The smell of Ben-Gay overpowered the room. Granny was lying on her side, reading the Bible, rubbing her left arm. Her hair was down and the bridge of her reading glasses rested low on her nose. "Can't sleep?" she asked.

"No, ma'am," I said.

She threw back the covers and I slipped into bed next to her. She kept rubbing her arm, making the flabby part above her elbow wave. Before turning off the lamp, she shut her Bible and put it with her glasses on top of the nightstand.

We lay there in the dark together with only the soft sound of Granny rubbing her skin and the smell of Ben-Gay tickling my nose. A couple of minutes later she said, "Your momma may have a simple mind, Tiger, but her love is simple too. It flows from her like a quick, easy river."

Her words soothed me and I soon fell asleep listening to her hand slide up and down her arm.

🐝　🐝　🐝

The next day, after I finished my chores, I went down to Saitter Creek to pick blackberries. For every five I plucked, I popped one into my mouth. Sweet juice coated my tongue and I thought how much sweeter they would taste in Granny's jam. Or if I picked enough, maybe in a blackberry pie.

Just as I filled berries up to the bucket's rim, I heard Momma scream. A scream that cut through me to the bone.

nine

I froze at the sight before me. Momma squatted in the garden, yelling, "No! Ma, no!" She bent over Granny, who lay near the butter bean vines.

Granny's wide-rimmed sunbonnet remained tied around her neck and her laced-up boots flattened vines beneath her. Her wire-framed glasses were clutched in one hand and a bucket of beans lay on its side near her feet.

Momma looked up at me, red faced and ugly. Her mouth opened and the words came out like glass cracking in tiny pieces. "My ma!"

Her mouth stayed open, but no other words came out. Only a low groan like I had once heard from a dog who had been accidentally shot in the leg.

I stood there stiff. My feet wouldn't step forward. My heart beat in my ears. I reeled around and ran to

Thompson's Nursery to fetch Daddy, taking the shortcut through the woods, dodging limbs, leaping over stumps. My chest felt heavy. Just breathing was difficult. My feet hit the path so hard I thought it would surely cause an earthquake.

At the nursery Mr. Thompson called for an ambulance in Alec, and Daddy and I drove to Dr. Randall's office near the sawmill. When we returned with Dr. Randall, Granny's sunbonnet was off. Momma was slumped with her head on Granny's bosom, and her hands clung to Granny's shoulders. Tears streaked Momma's cheeks as she sobbed loudly. "Ma! Talk to me!"

Daddy knelt next to Momma and ran his fingers through her hair.

"Don't touch me!" she snapped.

I jumped back the same time Daddy did. His face turned scarlet and he looked down at Granny.

Dr. Randall squatted next to Momma, his big belly hanging over his belt. He touched Granny's wrist, then dug out his stethoscope from his black leather bag and listened for a heartbeat. His temples pulsed. Slowly he pulled the stethoscope from his ears and let it rest around his neck.

Dr. Randall started to place a hand on Momma's

back but returned it to his lap. He looked up at Daddy, hesitated, then turned toward me. "It looks like Miz Jewel died from a heart attack."

"No," Momma whimpered.

Suddenly Daddy said, "Don't move, Corrina!"

Momma froze.

Then I saw it.

A coral snake coiled next to Granny's boot. Red, yellow, and black rings circled its body. Dr. Randall grabbed my wrist and together we stepped back slowly.

Momma jumped up and screamed, then yanked on Granny's arm, trying to drag her away from the snake. She pulled and pulled. But Granny's body only jerked up a little with each tug. Hairs from her bun shook loose and fell around her face.

The snake uncoiled and whipped toward Momma.

Daddy grabbed the hoe that lay on the ground and brought it down so quick I thought Granny would surely lose her foot. He brought the hoe down again and again, each time narrowly missing Granny's boot. In mere seconds Daddy had chopped the snake into pieces. Each part still wiggled, including the pointed head.

Daddy's eyes narrowed. He grabbed one of the

twisting pieces and shook it over his head, the blood dripping down his arm. "I got that old snake," he said.

Momma whimpered as she rocked Granny by the shoulders. Daddy threw the snake, piece by piece, toward the woods.

I just stood there. Frozen. I felt like I was watching a movie as I stared at Momma. Her long hair hid her face, the dark strands swaying as she rocked Granny.

From a distance I heard the whining sound of a siren coming closer. Closer and louder as it pierced my ears. I'd heard the sound before when Mr. Conners was taken to the hospital a year ago. It had scared me then, but now I felt numb. A moment later I saw the spinning red light on top of the ambulance approaching our driveway.

When the car stopped in front of our home, the noise vanished all at once, and two men dressed in white rushed out of the ambulance. Dr. Randall shook his head and motioned them over. He was whispering but I heard him say something about a funeral home. The men approached Granny, but Momma wouldn't let go of her. She sat with Granny's head in her lap, stroking her wrinkled face.

Dr. Randall squatted by Momma. "Corrina, I'm sorry, but we need to take your mother away."

Momma shook her head back and forth, her hands gripping Granny's collar. "No!" she yelled. "No, no, no!"

It took Daddy, Dr. Randall, and the two men to pry Momma away from Granny. She screamed, kicked, and punched. Finally they succeeded in wrestling Momma loose. They lifted Granny and placed her on a stretcher, then slid her into the ambulance. I quivered as I watched the double doors swing shut.

When the ambulance drove away, Momma ran, following them. Daddy raced after her. She tripped and fell. With a defeated look, Momma pounded the ground with her fists and watched the flashing light disappear down the lane. She sat there so still in the bright sunshine, whimpering. The sight of Momma tore a hole through my heart so big the Mississippi River could run through it.

Daddy's giant shadow approached Momma. He bent down and swept her up in his arms. This time she didn't fight. She rested her head on his shoulder as he carried her up the porch steps into the house.

Dr. Randall patted my back, walked to his car with hat in hand, and drove away. Smoke from his rusty Ford left a dissolving trail as it proceeded down our path. I felt so alone.

The excitement of the last hour was over. The

sound of Momma's screams and sobs. The sound of Daddy's hoe chopping the snake. The sound of the ambulance's siren. Quiet surrounded me. I felt hollow inside.

I stood under the huge oak tree watching the swing Daddy made from an old tire sway in the breeze. I remembered Granny pushing me in that swing as she hummed old Baptist hymns.

Only yesterday she showed me how to make the dumplings. I recalled her words. "It's time," she said. Had she known? Then I remembered how she had rubbed her left arm last night. I should have known that something was wrong with Granny, but I was too busy fretting about my problems.

I wanted to cry or do something, but I just stood there stunned. Nothing seemed real. If only I could close my eyes tight and count to ten and when I opened them Granny would be hollering, "Stop your daydreaming and get to work."

I closed my eyes. *One, two, three, four, five, six, seven, eight, nine, ten.* But when I opened my eyes the swing was still swaying and the butter bean vines were still mashed down in the spot where Granny fell. A shiver traveled down my spine and shook me to the core.

A few moments later a gentle touch on my arm caused me to look up. Brother Dave stood next to me under the oak. Then I noticed the rain. My hair and clothes were soaked, and I realized I was crying. Brother Dave opened his umbrella and raised it above our heads. "Come on, Tiger. Let's go inside."

Momma's bedroom door was open, and she lay curled up on her bed, sobbing. Brother Dave slowly closed the door, muffling Momma's cries.

Daddy paced the kitchen floor. He brushed his hair back with his hand as red wisps stubbornly fell back over his eyes. "What do you do, Brother Dave . . . when somebody dies?"

I wanted to yell, Why don't you know what to do, Daddy? Why aren't you like Mr. Thompson or other daddies?

Brother Dave placed a hand on Daddy's bony shoulder. "Lonnie, shouldn't you call Dorie Kay to let her know?"

My mind cleared. Finally there was something I could do. I dashed to the chest of drawers where the telephone book was kept and flipped open the inside cover. My trembling finger dialed the long-distance number. Then I handed Daddy the receiver.

Daddy's voice shook. "Dorie Kay, it's Lonnie. It's your ma, Dorie Kay. She was telling us last night on the porch how she needed to pick the rest of them butter beans."

Daddy didn't know how to tell a story without going to the very beginning. "When she got up this morning, she drank her coffee and said, 'Yes, sir. I need to get out there in the garden and finish picking those butter beans.' Then I had to go to work. Later in the day, when I saw Tiger come running like the dickens, I knew something was wrong. . . . What? . . . Tiger? Yes, she's right here. . . . Oh, all right."

Daddy offered the receiver to me. "Your aunt wants to talk to you, Tiger."

I could barely make my voice work. "Hello?"

Aunt Dorie Kay's tone sounded abrupt and impatient. "Tiger, what's wrong with Granny?"

I swallowed hard, not wanting to say the words. Afraid if I said the words, they would make it real. But this was real. "Granny's dead."

After a short pause she sighed. "I'll be up late this afternoon. Tell your momma and daddy I'll take care of everything."

After I hung up the phone, I thought how odd it was that Momma lay on the bed bawling her eyes out when Aunt Dorie Kay didn't seem sad at all. But I was relieved that my aunt's calmness would be with us shortly.

Barely an hour passed before our house filled with neighbors paying their respects with food. So many people.

Mr. Mayeaux had walked into the house, not bothering to wipe the dirt from his boots on the mat. My first thought was Granny was going to be real mad. Then I remembered.

Young children sat at their mothers' feet or in their laps. At that moment I wished so hard that I was small enough to crawl up in Momma's lap and rub her hair between my fingers. I stared at Momma's closed bedroom door.

Mrs. Thompson walked up and hugged me while Jesse Wade leaned next to the wall, looking at everyone in the room except me. "Oh, *ma chère*," she said softly. Her cool fingers touched my cheek as she held me next to her. Normally I would have welcomed Mrs. Thompson's hug. Today all I wanted to say was don't touch me, like Momma had snapped at Daddy earlier. But I didn't say anything, just waited the hug out like a wave releasing the shore.

Everyone said the same words. "I'm sorry about Jewel." "How's Corrina taking it?" "Is there anything we can do?"

Daddy always said the same thing too. "Dorie Kay said she'd take care of everything."

Every time I heard him say those words, I wanted to scream, "Why can't *you* take care of everything?"

Instead I walked out the front door. Jesse Wade followed me, and when I reached the gate, he covered his hand over mine. I yanked my hand and walked away.

Then I crept under the house with Brando. He wasn't much for showing affection, but somehow he must have known something was wrong. He rubbed his side against my leg and let me scratch behind his ear. A moment later he pranced off, as if like me, he couldn't tolerate too much touching.

From my hiding place, I waited for the last car to drive away. As I watched the Thompsons' car head on down the road, I wished I could turn back the clock and change things. I'd do things different. I'd forget about that stupid swimming party and never cry in front of Jesse Wade. Then he wouldn't have kissed me and I'd be playing baseball with him instead of snapping at him. And I'd watch Granny real careful. The first time she ever rubbed her arm, I'd call Dr. Randall to come out and check on her. He'd give her some medicine and then I wouldn't be squatting under the house like an old rat.

As I walked back into the yard, another car turned onto our dusty driveway. I couldn't handle any more tight hugs and soggy words so I dodged behind a lilac bush. When I realized Aunt Dorie Kay was the woman getting out of the car, I jumped out and dashed toward her.

Aunt Dorie Kay wore a yellow dress with a matching bolero jacket. When my dirty bare feet reached the toes of her yellow pumps she held out her arms and I fell into her embrace. Her *Evening in Paris* perfume floated in the air around us. I felt safe near her.

Walking arm in arm together toward the house, she softly said, "It's going to be all right now." And somehow I believed her.

She went straight into Momma's room and closed the door. Every once in a while I heard her soothing tone between Momma's sobs, but I couldn't make out the words.

While I listened to Momma cry, Daddy picked the rest of the butter beans in Granny's garden. He probably was thinking about how Granny never left a task undone.

Granny's apron hung over the arm of her chair. A lump clogged my throat. Walking over to the chair, I picked up the apron and stroked it against my cheek. The fabric smelled of Tabasco sauce and chicken and dumplings. Granny was gone. No one could listen to problems like she could. She listened with her heart as well as her ears.

Finally the door to Momma's dark room opened. Aunt Dorie Kay entered the living room, her yellow pumps dangling from one hand and a writing pad in the other. "Tiger, bring me the Alexandria telephone book."

I draped the apron over the chair's arm as I'd found it, then brought the telephone book to Aunt Dorie Kay.

She dragged a chair from the Formica table, positioned it near the phone, and started dialing. As soon as she hung up with one person, she crossed off his name on the pad and called another.

First she talked to the funeral home to set a time for choosing the casket. Next the newspaper for Granny's obituary. To my amazement, she rattled off the words without notes. She contacted Brother Dave to tell him when the funeral would be. My mouth hung open as I listened. No one ever told Brother Dave anything. They asked.

Then she ordered a spray of white carnations from the florist. Last she called the Jennings sisters to sing "Amazing Grace" at the funeral—Granny's favorite hymn.

My stomach growled, reminding me suppertime had arrived and I hadn't eaten lunch. A ham the Thompsons brought over was on the table next to Miz Eula's green beans and a couple of pies. I pulled the turquoise bowl out of the refrigerator and dished the chicken and dumplings into an iron Dutch oven. Daddy brought some wood in and heated up the stove.

When Aunt Dorie Kay finally hung up the last phone call, she sighed long and deep, rubbing the back of her neck. Her legs were bare, and her stockings scrunched up in her shoes. "Tiger, is that Ma's dumplings I smell?"

"Yes, ma'am. I have them on the table."

"Well, I'm starved. Let's eat."

Earlier, as I had stirred the dumplings, the lump in my throat grew as I thought of Granny stirring the same dinner the night before. But Aunt Dorie Kay acted like it was only another meal.

Once I told Granny how Darlie Reeves had acted at her mother's funeral. After the service people gathered at the graveyard, talking in soft voices as if not to wake the dead. Meanwhile Darlie played and laughed with some younger kids, darting around tombstones like they were trees on a playground. Granny had explained, "People handle death in different ways. Sometimes they act strange on the outside, but inside it's the same for everyone. Their hearts are breaking." Maybe the way Aunt Dorie Kay acted was her way of coping with a broken heart.

꽃　　　꽃　　　꽃

The next morning Momma didn't come out of her room. After breakfast Aunt Dorie Kay marched in and pulled up the shades. "Enough, Corrina. It's time to get up. There are things to do."

I stood near the door and peeked into the room. Poor Momma. How would she ever get by without Granny?

Momma covered her head with the sheets. "Ma's dead," she whimpered. "She went to heaven."

Aunt Dorie Kay faced the bed with hands on her narrow hips. "Yes, Corrina, Ma's dead. But you're not. And Lonnie's not. And I'm not. And neither is Tiger. What kind of mother lies in bed when she has a child to tend to? Do you think Tiger isn't hurting?"

White sheets slowly slipped below Momma's swollen face and tangled hair. Eyes peeped out like tiny slits in a stuffed bag. She sat up and her hand smothered cries as she rocked back and forth. She dropped her hand, allowing a sob to escape. "Oh, no! I've been bad. Tiger's going to be mad at me."

I ran into the room and settled next to her on the bed, surrounding her shoulders with my skinny arms. "I'm not mad at you, Momma. And you're not a bad mother. You've just been real sad."

We held each other a long time, rocking back and forth on that old feather bed. So long that Momma stopped crying, and Aunt Dorie Kay left the room to start on her busy list.

ten

I didn't cry at the funeral. I had to be strong for Momma and Daddy. In the coffin, Granny's white hands looked even paler next to the navy blue dress Aunt Dorie Kay sent her from Baton Rouge a year ago. Granny had never worn the dress before.

My heart had pounded with excitement the day Horace delivered the package containing the dress. Aunt Dorie Kay had included a petticoat for me. Only I didn't have any flared skirts to wear with it.

When Granny opened the package, her mouth curled as if she had taken a swallow of sour milk. "This dress is too fancy for Saitter," she said. "I wouldn't be caught dead in it." Large pearl buttons ran from the lacy white collar to the pleated hem.

The day before the funeral, Aunt Dorie Kay opened Granny's armoire and shuffled through the meager clothes hung there. Granny's calico dresses kept company beside her black skirt and white blouse for church. Aunt Dorie Kay's face stiffened when she discovered the navy blue dress with tags still attached, hung at the end of the row. I swear she aged twenty years in front of my eyes.

She yanked the dress out of the closet, then hunted for scissors in Granny's sewing basket. Her jaw tightened as she cut the strings. "It's the only decent thing she has to wear."

During the funeral Otis and his family stood at the back of the church. Minnie and Abner wore their Sunday clothes and Minnie wore new ribbons tied to her pigtails. Minnie's momma, Willie Mae, stood behind her, eyes fixed on the floor.

Outside the church Abby Lynn's mother steered her toward me. Abby Lynn stared over my left shoulder and mumbled, "I'm sorry about your granny."

After the funeral more people squeezed into our home than when Granny first died. They brought food, crying babies, and sympathy. Otis and his family were our only friends who weren't there.

Various dishes covered every inch of our kitchen table, forming a quilt of colors—glazed hams, smothered roasts, potato salad, cream gravy, cucumber salads, mustard greens, rice, and gumbo.

Desserts lay on top of the counter—buttermilk

pie, chocolate cake, fig cake, and blackberry cobbler. It looked like every woman in Saitter was competing for a blue ribbon at the fair.

Our neighbors had brought all this food, as if eating would fill up the big holes inside us. But eating was the last thing on my mind. I wanted to escape from the sad faces and hugging arms.

Aunt Dorie Kay stayed busy making chicory coffee and washing dishes with other women. When I tried to help, Mrs. Thompson said, "Tiger, that's okay. We've got these dishes under control."

Momma wept quietly on the couch. Miz Myrtle sat to her right, patting Momma's hand like a mother steadily burping a baby's back. On her left, Miz Eula sat with legs crossed at her skinny ankles. She patted Momma's knee. "There, there," she said over and over.

I wanted to yank Miz Eula's hand away and say, *"There, there."* Instead I left the room and stood on the porch in the miserable heat among women with crying babies in need of naps.

Hannah bounced Mr. Webster's wailing toddler on her hip, causing the baby's cries to vibrate. Hannah's face seemed as sad as ever.

Daddy stood in the front yard with some other

men. He kept his hands tucked in his pockets. Every once in a while a hand escaped its safe cubbyhole to sweep back the stubborn hair from his eyes.

Abby Lynn and the other girls sat under the mimosa tree giggling and whispering.

Each time anyone headed toward me, I'd casually turn and walk away, leaving them behind. Sometimes I couldn't dodge their words.

"Your granny was a wonderful lady."

"Your granny was a strong woman. When your granddaddy died, she didn't take handouts from anybody. She went out and got a job."

"Jewel was a good mother and grandmother. Lord knows she had enough tragedy come her way."

I slipped out the screened door and headed toward the creek. No one could tell me anything I didn't already know about Jewel Saitter Ramsey. The only thing I wished to hear, no one could say. I wanted to hear, "Wake up, Tiger, you must be having a bad dream."

Who would I share my worst days with? Granny could always put things in their right places, like the way she stored her canned vegetables and preserves. Neat and sensible. Most people stored their peas separately from their corn and their jellies. But Granny stored them huddled in mixed groups because we always cooked corn and peas on the same day we ate pickles and jelly. "That way you don't have to dig for them," she'd say.

It was the same way she'd tell me to stop worrying over something useless. "If you're gonna fret, fret over something you can change. Then stop fretting and do something about it."

Perched on a log, I watched gnats touch the water. A rustle from the bushes startled me.

"Tiger Ann?"

I gasped when I discovered Jesse Wade's reflection in the dark water. He stood directly behind me. Staring in the water, I asked, "What, Jesse Wade? What do you want now?"

I watched him turn his face toward the road as if someone might hear us. "I'm sorry, Tiger Ann. I shouldn't have kissed you. Not so soon anyway. I kind of sprung it on you."

"Sprung it on me? Jesse Wade, you never thought of me that way. Why did you have to go and ruin everything?"

"Tiger, how am I supposed to feel about you? You won't play baseball anymore. And you don't want me to kiss you. Do you just want me to disappear?"

"I don't want to talk about this right now."

"I know. I'm sorry about Miz Jewel. She was like a granny to me too."

I turned around and glared into his eyes until he shifted his gaze downward. "She wasn't your granny. She was mine. So leave me alone!" The moment I said those words, I regretted them, but something inside wouldn't let me take them back.

Jesse Wade looked hurt and puzzled. He turned and left. As he walked away, I watched him get smaller and smaller until he disappeared into the house. One part of me wished he would have stayed and another part of me was glad to see him go.

Hours passed like minutes as I sat near the creek, skipping pebbles across the water and smacking mosquitoes off my arms and legs. Back home, no one could see me because of the thick brush between the road and the creek, but I could watch the house through the branches.

Shortly after the last car left I heard Daddy holler, "Ti-ger!"

As I walked back to the house, I noticed the clouds were rolling in. The sky grayed as a sudden cool breeze warned of a summer storm. Daddy waited for me in front of the iron gate, his hands in his pockets. His hair blew wildly and his baggy pants waved around his thin legs.

As I neared, he pulled me toward him. His arms felt strong wrapped around me. "I'm sorry your granny died, Tiger. I'm so sorry."

For the first time that day, I cried.

eleven

The next day I sat on a stool in the kitchen while Aunt Dorie Kay showed Daddy how to write checks for the bills. She sat across from him at the table with a stack of envelopes between them.

In the beginning of their session, Aunt Dorie Kay's voice was kind and patient. "Now see. Everything is spelled out for you. It's really easy."

She demonstrated how to write a check for the bill's total, smiled at him, and said, "Your turn."

Daddy scratched his head as he picked up the bill. Confusion clouded his face. His hand brushed back his hair, still damp from washing. "I don't rightly see." His ears turned red, and I knew he was embarrassed.

Aunt Dorie Kay sighed. She spoke loudly, as if Daddy were hard of hearing. "Lonnie, the paper clearly shows the total amount. How could it be difficult?"

Daddy's ears turned redder. "But why do they give you all these numbers when they only want you to pay one of them? Seems like they want you to pay more than you have to."

Aunt Dorie Kay shook her head, then rested her forehead on her hands.

I sprang to my feet. "Show me how. I can take care of the bills." I wanted to save poor Daddy from his misery. He could tell us how many plant cuttings he'd made at work or how many eggs our hens laid. But if he faced numbers on paper, he'd freeze up.

Granny said Daddy's momma caused his fear of numbers. When his second-grade teacher had asked him why he couldn't finish his arithmetic, he put his hands in his pockets and said, "My momma says it's because I'm retarded."

Reading didn't come any easier for him. I remembered when I first started to read, he asked me, "Do them letters dance on the page?"

When I told him no, he looked relieved, smiled, and patted me on the head. "That's good," he had said. "That's real good."

Aunt Dorie Kay studied me a moment, then glanced at Daddy. He stared at the paper as if the total would pop out at him. Aunt Dorie Kay shook her head and sighed again. "You shouldn't have to worry about this, Tiger. You have plenty to do with your schoolwork."

Finally she gave up. She called Brother Dave, offering to exchange services. Daddy would mow the church lawn in return for Brother Dave writing out our monthly bills. I imagine most men would have been humiliated.

Daddy said, "I'd be happy to mow the church grounds for Brother Dave." Then he went out the front door whistling as he marched to the shed and took out the lawn mower. I stared at the floor. The pity I had for Daddy stirred with the shame I felt about him.

Aunt Dorie Kay hollered from the screened porch, "Lonnie, not right now. Starting next week." She stepped back into the kitchen with a worried look on her face.

Just then the phone rang and Aunt Dorie Kay answered. A moment later she said into the receiver, "I think that will do Tiger a world of good."

She saw me staring at her and added, "I know Tiger will want to help you, but I'll ask her to make sure."

After she hung up, she explained. "Woodrow

Thompson needs some extra help at the nursery for the rest of the summer. He's expecting big things with his Louisiana Lady camellias. He called to ask if you would like to work there. What do you think?"

I hoped it didn't mean Jesse Wade would see me. There was a big pit in my stomach because of everything I had said to him. But I heard myself answer, "I'd be glad to help out."

"I'll call him back," Aunt Dorie Kay said. "You'll get paid, of course. And it would keep your mind busy."

Later in the afternoon I lay on the couch reading while Momma watched cartoons from her pillow. Her hair was greasy and she smelled like sour milk. She had refused to take a bath or change out of her nightgown since the funeral.

Aunt Dorie Kay lifted my bare feet and settled beneath them. She wiggled one of my big toes. "Tiger, let's you and I go to a picture show in Alexandria."

"In Alec?"

"We could catch a matinee."

Movies were a rare treat. My feet hit the floor with a thump—"Yes, ma'am!"

⚜   ⚜   ⚜

The movie marquee read FUNNY FACE, STARRING AUDREY HEPBURN AND FRED ASTAIRE. We waited in the long line outside, listening to the popcorn machine in the lobby. Finally we reached the box office window and bought our tickets.

As we stood in the concession stand line, I noticed some colored people climbing the stairs to watch the movie from the second floor. Some of the little kids looked back at us in line.

In the dim auditorium we settled into the folding chairs facing the ruby curtains. I nibbled popcorn from a cardboard box and shared a large cola with Aunt Dorie Kay.

Before long the curtains opened to a giant silvery screen. My problems seemed to disappear as I focused on Miss Hepburn. She had a long neck like my own. Her slender shape didn't resemble the curvy figures of other movie stars, like Marilyn Monroe or Jane Russell. Maybe I wasn't doomed after all.

At the end of the movie I stood and stretched my arms above my head. "How about a milk shake?" Aunt Dorie Kay asked. She could turn plain days into holidays.

We strolled down the street to the drugstore soda

fountain. I sat on a stool in front of the shiny counter, watching the plump waitress scoop chocolate ice cream into tall mixing tumblers. Nearby some teenage girls wearing poodle skirts sat in a booth slurping Coke floats.

While I sipped my milk shake, a colored boy with curly eyelashes pressed his face against the window and watched me. I stopped drinking. A second later his mother snatched his hand and dragged him away.

The milk shake didn't taste so good after that. I looked around the drugstore. There were a lot of people. White people. I started thinking about all those colored folks climbing the stairs at the picture show while Aunt Dorie Kay and I sat on the first floor eating popcorn and slurping Coke.

I wanted to ask Aunt Dorie Kay about it, but I didn't want anything to spoil the afternoon. I felt proud to be with my sophisticated aunt. She wore real stockings. Every time her lipstick faded, she fetched the tube from her purse and reapplied a new coat without glancing in a mirror.

How would I survive in Saitter when she returned to Baton Rouge? After Abby Lynn's party, I didn't stand much of a chance of ever being close friends with her or any of the other girls.

I sucked the last drops of chocolate shake from the bottom of my fountain glass, wondering what would happen to me without Granny and Aunt Dorie Kay. Brother Dave would be doing the bills. But who would cook and clean and listen to my problems?

As I tried to stab the cherry with my straw, Aunt Dorie Kay swiveled on the stool and touched my arm. She spoke softly.

"Tiger?"

"Yes, ma'am?"

"How would you like to live with me in Baton Rouge?"

twelve

All I could think about on the ride home from Alec was living with Aunt Dorie Kay. A different school would give me a chance to make new friends. No one in Baton Rouge knew about Momma and Daddy.

"What's Baton Rouge like?" I asked.

"Oh, Tiger. You'll love it. The stores put Alexandria's to shame. And Louisiana State University is near my apartment. We could get tickets to a football game. You haven't seen football until you see the Fighting Tigers play."

I'd never seen any football game. Basketball and baseball were the only sports played in Saitter.

Aunt Dorie Kay gazed out the window as she drove along the highway. Her voice sounded dreamy when she spoke of Baton Rouge. For the first time I realized that she didn't think of Saitter as her hometown. She must have traded Saitter in for the excitement of Baton Rouge a long time ago.

"My apartment is a few minutes from downtown." She took a deep breath, then said, "I'll take you to the capitol and introduce you to my boss, Uncle Earl." Uncle Earl was a nickname for Governor Earl K. Long.

Aunt Dorie Kay continued, "Baton Rouge has beautiful parks. Maybe we can picnic at some of them."

She made everything sound like an adventure, but one thing weighed heavy on my mind. "What about Momma and Daddy? They aren't going to want me to leave them."

Aunt Dorie Kay glanced in the rearview mirror as she tapped her red fingernails on the steering wheel. "You leave that to me."

"But how will you convince them?"

She turned and drove over the railroad tracks, passing my school. "Well, for one thing, Tiger, if you lived with me you could go to a private school."

"Doesn't that cost a lot of money?" I swallowed, hoping my question didn't sound dumb.

She patted my head with quick gentle taps. "You don't need to worry about that. I have friends in the right places. This isn't a good time to tell your momma, though. We need to wait until she gets back on her feet. One step at a time, I always say. Meanwhile you stay busy working at the nursery, and I'm going to send Magnolia down here to help out."

"Who?"

"Magnolia, my colored maid. She'll be hard to convince, but maybe if she knows it's only for the summer. By then your momma should be back to norm—" She glanced my way. "Her regular self. I have an idea. How would you like to go back to Baton Rouge with me to get Magnolia? You could stay a couple of days and get a taste of your new life."

My new life. I loved the sound of those words. Then guilt faded my joy. "But what about Momma?"

"Miz Eula can look in on her in the day," she said, "and your daddy is home at night." I thought about Miz Eula's messy house and how Granny must be rolling in her grave. But there was nothing in the world I wanted more than to visit Aunt Dorie Kay in Baton Rouge.

"If you come," Aunt Dorie Kay said, "I'll show you the town." She smiled real big. I bet if the Gleem toothpaste people caught a glimpse of her pearly white teeth, they'd hire her on the spot to do a commercial.

I smiled back, running my tongue over my front teeth, checking for popcorn kernels.

She poked me gently in the ribs. "Stick with me, kid. I'll show you the ropes." She turned onto the winding path leading to our house and stopped the car in front of the mailbox. "Now be a dear and hop out and get the mail."

Everything seemed to be great for Aunt Dorie Kay when she had a mission. She bounced into our house so fast she nearly tripped over Momma, who was laying on the floor, wearing the same old gown, her head resting on her pillow as she watched television with sad eyes.

I held my breath as Aunt Dorie Kay made her announcement. "Guess what, Corrina?"

"What?" Momma managed to ask, keeping her eyes on the TV.

"You're going to have a visitor. My cleaning lady, Magnolia, is going to come and take care of you. Won't that be nice?"

Momma didn't say a word.

"She'll treat you like a queen. She'll cook your dinner, clean the house, and wash clothes."

Momma just stared at the set.

"And here's the best part. Tiger is going to go with me to pick her up."

Momma's eyes came to life and darted toward mine. I looked at the floor.

"Are you coming back?" she asked.

I swallowed. "Of course, Momma. I'm only going for a couple of days."

Aunt Dorie Kay brushed her hands together. "I'm going to call Miz Eula to look in on you. And I need to call Otis's wife. What's her name again?"

"Willie Mae," I said.

"Yes, that's right. I'm going to call Willie Mae to see if she knows a place where Magnolia can stay in the colored quarters. And then I'm going to call Miz Eula. Gracious, I hope that woman doesn't keep me on the phone yakking with her nonsense." Aunt Dorie Kay seemed to be talking to herself more than to us as she walked toward the kitchen. She was probably already making a new list in her head.

I knelt next to Momma and placed my hand on her greasy hair. "Momma? You know what I'd like to do before I leave with Aunt Dorie Kay? I'd like to wash your hair. Would you let me?"

"Uh-huh," she mumbled in her daze.

"The sun is shining so pretty today. We could wash it outside in the yard." I held out my hand and she slipped hers into mine. Finally she stood, all wobbly legged.

Outside, Momma sat in a chair with a washcloth covering her eyes. I warmed some well-water over the stove before pouring it over her head. The sun beat down on us as I worked the shampoo through her tangled hair. While white suds formed, I remembered something Brother Dave said about doing good deeds for the right reason. I wondered if I was washing Momma's hair because I wanted to do something good for her or if I was trying to feel less guilty about desperately wanting to leave Saitter.

As I finished rinsing her hair with vinegar, Aunt Dorie Kay came up to us. "It's all taken care of. Miz Eula will come by after Lonnie leaves for work. She said she'd be tickled pink to stay as long as she could watch her soap opera. Something about a wedding." Aunt Dorie Kay rolled her eyes. "And Willie Mae said there's a widow woman next door to them with a spare room."

Aunt Dorie Kay looked down at Momma as if seeing her for the first time this afternoon. "And now here's Corrina with squeaky clean hair. Didn't everything work out just fine?" Aunt Dorie Kay talked as if rinsing the soap off Momma made everything perfect.

I wrapped a towel around Momma's head, turban style. "Momma, would you like to take a bath now?"

Momma shook her head. "Na-uh."

Aunt Dorie Kay winked at me. "One step at a time, Tiger. One step at a time."

thirteen

The next day we loaded the car with Aunt Dorie Kay's two gray Samsonite suitcases and a paper sack that held my clothes. Momma and Daddy stood side by side, Momma's hands folded together in front of her. I wanted to remember Momma pretty, but her face was swollen from all the crying last week, and she still wore that grimy nightgown. Daddy wrapped his arm around her shoulders as if to warm her, despite the June heat.

Aunt Dorie Kay brushed her palms together. "Well, I guess that's it, Tiger. Everything is in the car."

Aunt Dorie Kay hugged Momma. "Don't you worry, Corrina. I'll take good care of her. She'll be back before you know it. All right?"

Momma nodded, her lips pressed tight.

Aunt Dorie Kay offered her a smile and patted her arm. Then she got in the car and waited.

I hugged Momma.

She opened her mouth enough to gasp for air and a sob escaped. Then she closed her lips tightly again. As she held me snugly, the smell of her shampoo reminded me of when she used to sing me a song she had made up. *"Momma's got a little baby. Momma's got a little child. Momma's got a little Tiger, who makes her momma smile."* I had forgotten that song and those rocking chair days. Until now.

I gently pulled away from her and turned to Daddy. His hands popped out of his pockets and he reached out, drawing me against him. His unshaven cheek felt rough next to my forehead. "You're my special girl, Tiger. Don't you forget it."

A giant lump caught in my throat and I nodded. Aunt Dorie Kay was the only one who could speak. As I got in the car she called out, "Good-bye. Don't worry about a thing. She'll be fine."

The car's tires crunched rocks below as we pulled away from the driveway. While she drove down the lane, I turned and waved at Momma and Daddy. Momma's hands stayed locked together, but Daddy waved back.

Aunt Dorie Kay flicked the car radio on and Hank Williams sang, "I'm so lonesome I could die." She quickly turned the dial and "Rock Around the Clock" came on. She stayed quiet, as if she knew I needed time to adjust. For miles the radio filled the silence in the car.

We soon passed the sick-sweet smell of the sugar-cane mills in Lecompte, and a half hour later we reached Bunkie. Aunt Dorie Kay drove up to a gas station. "I need to buy some gasoline. How about a soda pop and a candy bar?"

"That sounds good."

While the gas station attendant filled the tank, Aunt Dorie Kay dashed inside the station. She returned with two bottles of cola and a Baby Ruth. After the man cleaned off the windshield, she paid him, and we headed back onto the highway. I let the chocolate melt slowly in my mouth, saving the peanuts to crunch on last.

Excitement perked inside me as we left the town limits of Bunkie. I had never been past Bunkie before. Everything from there on would be a new adventure.

Miles stretched out before us on Highway 71. We passed houses with children playing in their yards, sugarcane farms with colored folks gathering crops, and an occasional gasoline station.

I leaned against the passenger door and watched Aunt Dorie Kay drive as she hummed to the radio. She and Momma were as different as midnight and noon. I watched Aunt Dorie Kay press her red lips together and thought about how they reacted so differently to Granny's death.

Aunt Dorie Kay must have felt me studying her because she glanced my way and asked, "What?"

I blushed. "Nothing, I was only thinking."

"Thinking about what?"

I swallowed, hunching my shoulders. "Do you miss Granny?"

She gazed straight ahead. "I lost Ma a long time ago."

"What do you mean?"

She turned her face slightly toward me. "I love your momma, Tiger, but it wasn't easy being her sister. I was five years younger than her, but I had to act like the oldest." Her voice tightened like she was trying to hold back anger. "I had responsibilities your momma never had.

"Boys didn't date me because of my strange sister. They were afraid it ran in our family. But Corrina wasn't born that way." She glanced at me and blushed. "Oh, I'm sorry, Tiger. Here I am talking as if Corrina wasn't your momma. Please forgive me. I love her dearly. You know that."

The chocolate soured in my stomach. "Momma wasn't born *slow*?"

Aunt Dorie Kay went white. "I shouldn't have said that." She tapped her red fingernails on the dashboard. "Let's talk about something more pleasant, shall we?"

We talked about Baton Rouge, but one question spun around and around in my head—*What had happened to Momma?*

Late morning heat caused us to roll down our windows. My pigtail slapped my back while wisps blew around my face. Aunt Dorie Kay stopped the car on the edge of the road and tied a scarf around her head. "Would you like a scarf?"

A few minutes later we were back on the road— a beige scarf around Aunt Dorie Kay's head and a charcoal-gray one around mine. It was funny how a scarf made me feel sophisticated and a sunbonnet made me feel goofy.

About forty miles outside of Bunkie, swamps and bayous began to replace the pine trees. We passed a

shack with a sign that read BATE FOR SALE. I wondered if anyone ever told the person who wrote that
sign that they spelled *bait* wrong.

About twenty minutes later I caught a glimpse of
the capitol building. The city looked like a dark
stitch on the horizon.

Aunt Dorie Kay cleared her throat. "Before we
reach the city, I need to talk to you about something.
It's really nothing, but I don't go by Dorie Kay in
Baton Rouge."

"You don't?"

"No. I go by my given name, Doreen. I'd like you
to call me that too, please."

"Oh, okay. It may take me a while, but I'll try
real hard."

She smiled. "Thanks. I knew you'd understand."
After pausing for a moment she asked, "Hey, have
you ever thought about going by your middle name?"

I shrugged.

"Think about it. Tiger's a darling name, but I'm
afraid you might have a hard time with it in Baton
Rouge."

I was moving to get away from a hard time. I sure
didn't want to meet another one in Baton Rouge.
Still, it seemed strange to think of myself as Ann.

"Ann Parker." Aunt Dorie Kay said the name as if she were trying on a hat to see if it fit. "Sounds like a movie star."

It sounded plain to me. But a plain name was better than being teased.

Aunt Dorie Kay smiled as she watched the road in front of her. "We could practice using it on this short trip. Only if you want to, though." She peered sideways at me. "You can reinvent yourself in Baton Rouge, Tiger. That's what I did. Whoever thought a country bumpkin like me from Saitter could make it in a city like Baton Rouge?"

She looked at me, waiting like she wanted me to say something. "You know how I did it?"

"How?" I asked.

"When I moved here nine years ago, I practiced voice patterns of women on radio commercials, studied fashion magazines for the latest styles, and put myself through secretarial school. Would you believe I graduated at the top of my class?"

I smiled at her. Aunt Dorie Kay must have wanted to reach for the moon, like me.

She drew a deep breath. "Sometimes I shudder when I think about what I used to look like. That awful hairdo I wore before I went to a Baton Rouge beauty shop. Say, have you ever thought of cutting your braid?"

"Not really." I pictured Momma brushing my hair at night on the porch and Daddy playfully yanking it.

She waved her hand as if she were swatting a fly. "Oh, it's pretty the way it is. Don't listen to me. I love to make improvements."

I wondered what else about me needed improving. Was I going to fit in in Baton Rouge? Could a hundred miles make that much difference? At least I had someone worldly like Aunt Dorie Kay to help me.

When we crossed the Mississippi River Bridge, I held my breath. The only bridges I'd ridden on were small ones, stretching over creeks. The Mississippi was wider than any creek or bayou I'd seen. Tugboats and barges were scattered about on the black water below us.

On the other side of the river tall buildings touched the sky, cars filled the streets, and people bustled everywhere. My mouth dropped open, and my head darted in every direction. Right, left, then in back of me. I tried to catch all the excitement before it disappeared.

Aunt Dorie Kay laughed. "Welcome to Baton

Rouge, Ann Parker. Welcome to your new home."
It was as if what she said about Momma an hour
ago hadn't been mentioned. But it had, and I knew
I would never be the same until I found out what
she meant.

When we drove past the university, she said,
"Maybe you can attend college here one day."

About a mile off campus we pulled into a parking
lot in front of a round two-story building with a
dome on top. "This is it," she said. "This is my
apartment."

The sidewalk led us to the inside of the building.
Each apartment's sliding glass door faced the swim-
ming pool stretched out in the center of a courtyard
filled with plants. I felt like I'd stepped right into an
Audrey Hepburn movie. Eat your heart out, Abby
Lynn Anders!

The apartment smelled like fresh paint. Aunt
Dorie Kay drew the pleated drapes and sunlight
brightened the living room. The courtyard view
turned the sliding glass door into a huge picture.
Turquoise and pink pillows perked up the cream sofa
by the coffee table.

Her bathroom was all pink—even the tub.

"Look at this," she said, turning on the faucet.

Running water poured from the opening. No more trips to the well or taking a bath in that old aluminum tub on the porch.

"If you want, you can take a bubble bath tonight," she said. "Come on, I'll show you your room."

At the end of a short, narrow hall, she opened a door to a white room. In the center was a bed covered with a chenille spread trimmed in pink roses. An oak dresser and matching nightstand faced the bed. She opened the blinds and plumped up a toss pillow.

I pinched my arm to make sure I wasn't dreaming. "Will this be *my* room?"

Aunt Dorie Kay smiled. "Yes, Tig—I mean Ann, this is your room. Do you like it?"

"Like it? I love it. It's like a movie star's room."

She patted my arm and said, "I'll leave you alone to unpack and get comfortable."

I emptied the brown paper sack and placed my clothes in the dresser drawers, then tucked the envelope of money Daddy gave me under my nightgown in the bottom drawer. Framed photos lined the top of the dresser. I recognized the one of me at seven with my two missing teeth. Another showed a young Granny and Granddaddy standing on the porch. I never knew Granddaddy because he died when Momma and Aunt Dorie Kay were young, but Granny said he was always making people laugh. In the picture he was smiling like he just told a joke. Granny stood tall and proud next to him, frowning as she always did in pictures.

Two children in the last photo smiled back at me—a wispy-haired toddler and a pretty dark-haired girl who looked to be about six years old. The older girl's arm wrapped around the little girl. I slid the picture out from the frame and held it near the window's light. On the back of the picture the names Corrina and Doreen Kay Ramsey and the year, 1925, were penciled in Granny's handwriting.

I had never seen a picture of Momma as a child. It seemed so odd to stare into her face. Something was different about her in that picture. Maybe the way she had her arm around Aunt Dorie Kay— so protective-like. The way I wished she would protect me.

Just then Aunt Dorie Kay poked her head into my new room. "Finished?" Her smile faded when she saw me looking at the snapshot. She came over, sat down next to me, and gently took the picture from my hand.

For a long moment she said nothing. She just

stared at the photo. Finally she spoke, her words spilling out slowly. "When I was a toddler, I climbed on everything. Ma said I was like a cat. Even though Corrina was barely six years old, she followed me around like a mother hen."

"Momma?"

"That's right. One day your granny left a ladder leaning against the oak tree after she finished trimming some limbs. I climbed up to the top step and held on to a branch." Aunt Dorie Kay stayed quiet for a long moment, then continued. "Your momma went up after me, but as she reached for me, she fell back to the ground. She broke her arm, but her head took the worst hit. It was like her mind wouldn't go past that day. Doctors said she'd probably always be like a six-year-old. I think Ma never forgave herself for leaving that ladder out, or me for climbing up the tree."

"But you were a baby. It wasn't your fault."

Aunt Dorie Kay didn't say anything. She just looked down at that picture.

"Why didn't anyone ever tell me?" I asked.

Aunt Dorie Kay shook her head. "I don't know. Someone should have. Granny never even touched the subject with me except once. I was a teenager and frustrated because I had to take Corrina everywhere I went after school." Aunt Dorie Kay looked out the window. "I'm ashamed to say I was embarrassed by my sister. Of course after Granny told me what happened, I had tremendous guilt."

I felt like I should say something, but I didn't know what to say. My mind was stuck on Momma, and wondering what life would be like today if she hadn't fallen. Maybe instead of Aunt Dorie Kay, my own momma would be sitting next to me wearing red lipstick and smelling like Evening in Paris perfume. It was as if all my questions had been answered in one big sweep. Now I knew how I could be on the honor roll and why Granny had seemed so hard on Aunt Dorie Kay. But I hoped it wasn't because of guilt that Aunt Dorie Kay had asked me to live with her.

Aunt Dorie Kay placed the photo back in the frame, then returned it to the dresser. She swirled around with a smile that almost startled me. "Let's go shopping."

I guess telling me about Momma was like crossing another task off her list.

"Grocery shopping?" I asked.

"No. The dresses your momma and Granny were

sewing are sweet, but Corrina will never finish making them. Let's buy some clothes Ann Parker from Baton Rouge would wear."

My head felt dizzy. Momma had lived a whole life that I didn't even know about. Everyone had kept it a secret. As far as I knew, the whole town of Saitter knew what had happened to Momma. Maybe Jesse Wade's momma had even told him.

After slipping on my shoes, I followed Aunt Dorie Kay down the hall, out of the apartment, and toward her car. She was right. She sure did like to make improvements.

Two hours later I was the proud owner of four new blouses and three skirts. A pink one even had a poodle on it like Abby Lynn's. Aunt Dorie Kay also bought lots of petticoats to make my skirts flare out. The dresses Momma and Granny had started looked childish compared to my new wardrobe.

I modeled the pink skirt in front of the mirror, feeling like a new person. I kind of looked like one of those teenagers I saw drinking Coke floats at the drugstore instead of some country bumpkin feeding chickens in Saitter. *Good-bye, Tiger. Hello, Ann Parker.*

fourteen

The next morning I awoke to the smell of fried ham and an unfamiliar voice singing off-key. I stumbled into the kitchen and saw a tiny woman, barely five feet tall, standing at the stove. Her skin was the color of coffee and she wore her gray hair in a bun like Granny.

She sang a gospel song I had never heard before. The words squeaked out of her in the high parts and went flat in the low notes.

With her backside to me she said, "Good morning, Ann. You want some breakfast?"

I gasped. "Yes, ma'am." When I was younger, Granny had convinced me she had eyes in the back of her head. She always knew when I was up to mischief. I eventually decided she had a sixth sense. Maybe this woman possessed it too.

Keeping her back to me, she flipped thick ham slices in an iron skillet. Then she stepped on a footstool, opened a cabinet, and reached for a jar of fig preserves. "Have you washed? No, s'pect you haven't. Go wash. Then you can eat."

When I returned from my morning scrubbing, she had set a place at the table. I stared down at a plate of fried ham, grits, and biscuits.

She turned, facing me. She had smooth skin and high cheekbones and her caramel eyes sparkled when she spoke. "My name's Magnolia." Her voice was frail and a little scratchy like a record that had been played again and again.

"Pleased to meet you." The buttery grits in my mouth were a fair match to Granny's. "Where's Aunt Dori—Aunt Doreen?"

Magnolia seemed to catch my slip and smiled. "She's working, honey. She's a working girl. I guess you could say I'm *her working girl*." She chuckled, then added, "But I'm no girl, am I? Sixty-five years old. Did your aunt tell you I'd be coming today?"

I swallowed a bite of ham and washed it down with a swig of milk. "No, ma'am."

Her tongue snapped against the roof of her mouth as she shook her head. "Busy, busy. Always too busy.

She works hard, though. I'm your aunt's cleaning lady. Some nights I make her supper too. When she isn't going out."

"Going out?" I asked.

"You know, she goes to a lot of fancy parties for the governor. Funny how it take a whole lot of money to get a man a job that don't pay that much." She reminded me of Granny—suspicious.

Magnolia squirted some dish soap in the sink and turned on the water. Her face grew serious. "I guess me and you be seeing a lot of each other this summer. Your people ain't fussy folks, are they?"

"Oh, no, ma'am."

"Good, 'cuz I can't take no fussy eaters. I make one dinner for everybody. That's it."

"We eat almost anything."

"Good. And don't get too used to my ole face 'cuz as soon as I can, I'm a-headin' home. Didn't sign on for no long trip." I wondered how Aunt Dorie Kay had convinced her to go at all.

I offered to help wash the dishes, but Magnolia insisted on doing them herself. "Your aunt pay me to do the cleaning. If I don't do it, then there won't be no chicken in my pot."

I changed to my swimsuit and dashed to the pool.

The water was different from the creek—warm and funny tasting. Floating on my back, I gazed at the sky through the see-through dome. The palm trees and ferns made me feel like I was smack in the middle of a postcard from Hawaii. I wished Abby Lynn could see me, floating in a glamorous swimming pool in Baton Rouge. She'd be as jealous as green pea soup.

An admiring whistle from an apartment above woke me from my daydream. I glanced around, trying to act unshaken by the intruder. At least a hundred windows faced the pool, but not one had a person looking out. I swam a few more minutes, but the fun was gone. I kept wondering who was peeping at me. I decided to dry off and return to the apartment.

Magnolia washed and dried the clothes a few doors down in the complex's laundry room. Her determination to do the chores alone left me with a lot of time to stretch out on my bed and read a bunch of Aunt Dorie Kay's movie magazines. An article in *Screen Stars* about Audrey Hepburn caught my attention. The article mentioned Miss Hepburn's "unique physical appearance."

I looked in the dresser mirror, gathering my hair

behind my head. Maybe I should get my hair cut. Then maybe I would look glamorous. I pretended to apply lipstick like Aunt Dorie Kay, pursing my lips like a kiss. Then I remembered Jesse Wade and wiped my mouth with my sleeve.

In the living room Magnolia stood with her feet apart as she flung open each towel, then folded it in half. "If you're bored," she said, "you can go run to the post office for me. Your aunt needs her bills mailed and she's out of stamps."

"Where's the post office?"

"Up the road a few blocks and across the street. Be careful, child. This ain't the country."

"Don't worry. I'll be right back." Before leaving, I took a few dollars from the envelope Daddy gave me and tucked them in my pocket.

Passing cars buzzed by as I followed the side-walk to the shopping area. Stores lined both sides of the street. The post office was tucked in between LeBlanc's Hat Boutique and Hazel's Beauty Shop.

After buying stamps, I dropped the bills through a slot that read In Town and walked back into the morning heat. Pictures of women with stylish hair-dos smiled from the beauty shop window next door. A price list posted in the window showed that a haircut cost two dollars. There was enough money left over from the stamps to do what I had been thinking about.

Bells jingled when I opened the door. A platinum blond lady was tightly rolling another woman's gray hair in curlers. The beautician looked at my reflection in the mirrored wall. "Hi. Haircut or wash and roll?"

I gulped. "Haircut," I said too loud. I scanned the room, as if Momma or Daddy would pop out from behind a closed door.

"I'm Hazel. Sit down and I'll be with you in a sec. If you like, you can thumb through those magazines and see if there's a hairdo you want. If you find a picture, I can copy it. I can copy anything from a picture." She smacked her chewing gum and continued rolling the lady's hair.

I searched through a pile of magazines until I found the same issue of *Screen Stars* as Aunt Dorie Kay's, showing Audrey Hepburn's short hairdo. I studied the picture close. Yes, it was short. Yes, I wanted to do this.

Hazel guided the woman with curlers to the side of the room where hair dryers lined the wall. Then she directed me to another chair in front of a sink, wrapped a towel around my shoulders, and undid my braid. She raked a brush through my hair, yanking out the tangles. "Gracious, this must be a lot of trouble to keep up." Then she tugged on a black rubber hose with a sprayer and said, "Lean back."

She bent over and sprayed cold water on my head before squirting on the shampoo.

I could smell the spearmint gum in her mouth and strong chemicals from her pink jacket. My eyes watered as her fingers dug into my scalp and scrubbed viciously. Sometimes Momma shampooed my hair, but she washed gently. My head ached but I was afraid to say anything since Hazel was about to cut my hair.

Finally she rinsed it with warm water, wrapped a towel around my scalp, and led me to a chair in front of the mirrored wall. "That's a lot of hair. Are you sure you want to cut it?"

"Yes, ma'am. I'm sure."

"Okay. Well, what can I do you for?"

I held up the picture. "Can you do something like this?"

Smacking her gum, she said, "Hepburn, huh? I can do that blindfolded." She opened a squeaky drawer and pulled out her scissors.

I closed my eyes and held my breath. *Snip.* I took a quick peek in time to watch a long lock of hair near my face fall to the floor.

"Have you ever had your hair cut?" Hazel asked.

"No, ma'am. Well, Granny trimmed my hair on full-moon days."

She stopped cutting and I saw her eyebrows shoot up in the mirror. "What?"

"Full-moon days. If you trim your hair when there's a full moon, it grows faster."

She bent at the waist and cackled. "I never heard of such a thing. Where are you from?"

I turned red. "Saitter."

"Well, Miss Saitter, don't go telling anyone around here that story." She snipped and snipped while I closed my eyes.

About twenty minutes later she said, "You can look now. I'm finished."

Slowly I opened my eyes and searched for Audrey Hepburn. My face appeared bigger under the short style, like somebody wearing a hat too small for their head. My nose stood out and my eyes shrank to small slits.

"You look great," she said. "Glamorous. A little like Audrey Hepburn." She picked up a comb and started touching up her own hair.

I stared at my face. Maybe shock kept me from seeing what she saw. On the floor my hair lay in batches like red straw.

Hazel gazed out the window, chewing her gum. With a hand on her hip, she said, "That little colored woman has been standing outside, staring this way for the last twenty minutes. There isn't any bus stop there."

I glanced out the window and recognized Magnolia on the sidewalk across the street. Wearing a gray pillbox hat, she stood under the shade of a red umbrella, looking toward the beauty shop.

"Oh, no!" I said.

"What?" Hazel asked.

"I better go. How much do I owe you?"

"Two dollars, but your hair's wet. Don't you want to sit under the dryer?"

"It'll dry at home." I handed two crumbled bills to Hazel and hurried out the door. The bell's jingle faded as I dashed across the street, forgetting to look both ways. A car honked and screeched to a halt inches from me. Then the car behind him honked too. My head pounded as horns kept sounding. I froze, not knowing which way to go.

"Oh, Lawd!" Magnolia cried.

The angry driver impatiently waved his hand

toward the sidewalk, and I raced across to Magnolia's side.

She shook her head, her eyes fixed on my hair. "Good grief, child. I was worried about you when you didn't come right back from that post office. Now I'm worried about me. Your aunt is gonna kill me."

I ran my fingers through my wet short locks. "She wanted me to get my hair cut."

Magnolia walked at a quick pace in front of me, her red umbrella dancing above her. "Mmmm-mmm-mmm-mmm-mmm." She shook her head. "At least you done cut it on a full-moon day."

fifteen

An hour after Magnolia left to ride the bus home, Aunt Dorie Kay buzzed into the apartment and dropped her purse when she set eyes on me. "Your hair! I love it!"

I tugged at my short strands. "You do? Really? You don't think my nose looks too big?"

"No, not at all. It gives you class. You look every bit of thirteen. Maybe even fourteen."

I resisted the urge to dash to the mirror and study my face. Again. When I checked earlier, all I saw was a redheaded, squinty-eyed, big-nosed girl. Maybe I needed glasses.

Later Aunt Dorie Kay grilled hamburgers outside in the courtyard while I fried sliced potatoes in butter over the electric stove. To my amazement, it turned on with a twist of the dial. I felt so grown-up thinking about what my new life would be like in Baton Rouge.

I wondered why Aunt Dorie Kay wasn't married. Miz Eula had often asked Granny, "You reckon Dorie Kay plans on being an old maid?"

At the dinner table I asked, "Do you have a boyfriend?"

Aunt Dorie Kay dabbed a french fry in a pool of ketchup. "I'm so busy working, no man would want me." I wondered if that meant she wouldn't have time for me either.

"But don't worry," she said. "I go out every now and then." She wiped her mouth with her napkin even though it was already clean. "Why do you ask? Or did Granny mention it?"

"Oh, no, not Granny. Miz Eu—"

She tossed her head back and laughed. "Oh, yes, Miz Eula! How would Saitter survive without old nosy Miz Eula? Tell you what, next time Miz Eula asks about me, you tell her I'm doing just fine. That somehow I even manage to pay my bills all by my itty-bitty self."

"That's what Granny always told her."

Her face grew serious. "Really?"

"Yes, ma'am. Granny would say, 'One thing I

don't have to worry about is my gal Dorie Kay. She's got a good head on her shoulders.' "

Aunt Dorie Kay bit her lower lip and tears filled her eyes. She lifted her water glass to her mouth and didn't put it down until it was empty. As I listened to giant gulps slide down her throat, I decided I probably shouldn't have told her what Granny had said. It seemed to make her sad.

After we finished dinner, I drew hot water in the sink, and we washed dishes together, listening to the radio. When Elvis came on, Aunt Dorie Kay said, "Now, that's a man. I'd leave my job in a heartbeat for him."

We dropped the dishcloths and danced, our bare feet slapping the linoleum floor. Aunt Dorie Kay mouthed the words into a wooden spoon. *"Let's rock. Everybody, let's rock."* She twisted her lower body to the beat of the music—just like Elvis, then grabbed my hand and twirled me around the room.

The song ended and we laughed so hard Aunt Dorie Kay slipped in a puddle of water in front of the sink. I stopped laughing, but Aunt Dorie Kay sat there on the floor, her legs stretched out in front of her, laughing with mascara running down her face in black streaks. Maybe Aunt Dorie Kay was finally letting those tears loose for Granny.

"Oh, mercy," she said, wiping her eyes with her fists. "Mercy, mercy." I handed a dishcloth to her and she wiped her face, spreading the mascara even more. "I bet I look a fright, don't I? I better go and wash up."

I was sweeping the floor when Aunt Dorie Kay returned wearing a loose pair of pants. With her face free of makeup, she looked so young—almost like one of those college girls we passed by on the LSU campus.

As she shoved the kitchen chairs in place she asked, "Is there anybody special that you'll miss when you move here?"

"Do you mean Momma and Daddy?"

"Of course you'll miss them. But how about Jesse Wade? He sure is a cute thing."

My stomach rumbled and my face burned. "Oh, him. He's just a friend. I guess he's still a friend."

"What do you mean?"

"Oh, nothing."

She gently nudged me in the ribs with her elbow. "Come on. You can tell your future roommate."

I really did want to tell her, but it was embarrassing. Finally I blurted, "He kissed me."

"Whooo-wee! Your first kiss?"

I nodded.

Her fingers brushed my bangs. "Everyone has a first kiss."

"You don't understand. I don't like him that way. I yelled at him and told him to leave me alone. I think he thinks I meant forever."

"Oh, dear," she said, rubbing her chin.

"I wish I could take it back."

"Then do it," she said.

"But I don't want him to think I want to be his girlfriend."

"Tell him that too. But also tell him you need his friendship." She grabbed hold of my shoulders. "Tiger, you'll regret it if you don't. Believe me, I know."

"Did the same thing happen to you?"

"Not a boy." She turned her back to me and wiped up the soapy splashes around the sink. "Ma."

"Granny?"

"I wanted so much to show Ma I loved her, but she never accepted me living away from Saitter. I think Granny expected me to stay in Saitter to take care of Corrina. After she realized I had left for good, she allowed your daddy to marry Corrina. I'm sure she was convinced I thought Saitter wasn't good enough for me. But I just wanted more from life."

She turned back around, facing me. "Is that so wrong?" She was asking me, but I got the feeling the question was for Granny. She looked so fragile standing there in those baggy pants, I put my arms around her.

"I wish I told her what she meant to me. I would never have had the courage to strike out on my own if it weren't for Ma. She was strong—the way she raised us on her own after Poppa died. I grew up knowing that if you want something done, do it yourself." Aunt Dorie Kay smiled and changed her voice to an upbeat tone. "So learn from your foolish aunt. Okay? Promise me you'll talk to Jesse Wade."

"I promise."

She took a deep breath. "I hope Magnolia won't get all uppity on y'all. I had to practically promise her the moon to convince her to go to Saitter."

🌺 🌺 🌺

Next morning I packed my new clothes in one of Aunt Dorie Kay's suitcases and we drove to Roosevelt Street to pick up Magnolia.

On Magnolia's street, smells of fried foods mixed with the scent of roses. Small worn-down houses lined the street. Little girls jump-roped on the sidewalks. Boys dressed in white T-shirts and cuffed jeans chased each other, laughing as they ran. Adults sitting on porches talked to folks across the road. Maybe it wouldn't be so bad living with your neighbors' houses all crowded next to each other. I wondered if this was what the colored quarters in Saitter were like.

We drove to the end of the street and parked in front of a blue house with a yellow front door. Birdhouses perched on posts through the yard and a small windmill stood motionless. Giant yellow and orange zinnias grew wild around the fence.

Magnolia sat on the porch step, wearing her gray hat, holding a brown paper sack with her umbrella poking out from the top. A young man stared between the curtains, but when he saw me looking at him he let go of the panels. Magnolia walked toward us and I started to get out of the car, but Aunt Dorie Kay grabbed my shirttail.

"Don't get out *here*," she whispered. It reminded me of when Granny wouldn't let me go with Daddy to help fix Otis's roof. I had wanted to see Minnie and Abner's house in the colored quarters, but Granny had said, "You don't need to be going down that way. Best you stay home."

When we arrived at the bus station, Aunt Dorie

Kay placed her hands on my shoulders. "Now remember, I'll return for you at the end of the summer. Baton Rouge will be your new home."

Magnolia frowned, her eyebrows touching, but when she saw Aunt Dorie Kay look at her, she glanced toward the bus, pulling up to the station. "Don't worry, Magnolia," said Aunt Dorie Kay. "I'll return for you soon."

A voice on an intercom said, "Departure for Alexandria and all destinations in between."

Although I rode a bus to school, I had never ridden on a big Greyhound bus. When the bus door whished open we stepped on and I selected a seat close to the front, scooting over next to the window to make room for Magnolia. Instead she walked to the back of the bus and an old man in overalls sat next to me.

"How are you, young lady?" he asked. His breath smelled like he'd eaten a bowl of gumbo with lots of onions.

I answered, "Just fine, sir."

"Did'ja say you needed a dime?" He dug into his pocket and pulled out a bunch of change, then handed me a couple of dimes. "Here, have two."

"No, sir. Thank you."

With a shrug he returned one of the dimes to his pocket, still holding out the other to me.

I didn't know what else to do but take it. "Thank you."

He nodded. "Going home?" he asked.

"Yes, sir."

He leaned over, cupping his ear with a hand. "Huh?"

"Yes," I repeated, this time louder.

"Where's home?"

"Saitter."

He wrinkled his forehead. "Tater? Like the potato? Can't say I've heard of it."

Behind me I heard someone's muffled laugh. It sounded like Magnolia. I leaned into his ear and yelled, *"Saitter!"*

He leaned back. "Don't have to holler; I'm not deaf. Saitter. That's where those two big nurseries are, ain't it?" If he kept asking me questions, this was going to be a long ride.

It *was* a long ride. The bus not only stopped for people, but the driver also delivered packages.

Two and a half hours later we reached Bunkie and the old man stood, tucking his thumbs under his overall straps. "Don't you worry about paying that dime back."

By then the bus had cleared out except for some young army man who was going home to Alec. I walked to the back of the bus and plopped in a seat in front of Magnolia. This time I slid over to the middle, making sure nobody else would sit next to me. I turned around and asked, "Do you have any children?"

Magnolia stared out the window. "I got a son. His name's Michael." He must have been the man I saw looking out the window.

"How old is he?"

"Twenty-six next month. I guess I'll miss his birthday this year. First time ever." She continued looking out the window.

"What kind of work does he do?"

"He don't have a job." Her dark eyes met mine. "These days the world is a hard place for a young Negro man to live."

"What do you mean?" I asked.

She lowered her eyebrows. "Do your folks know you planning to live with your aunt?"

I swallowed. "Not yet." I turned back around and opened my book but her question burned in my mind.

A few miles south of Saitter, small trees turned

into tall pines lining the road, welcoming me back home. My heart leaped when I saw Daddy, a straw hat on his head and hands tucked in his pockets. I had hoped Momma would be there too, but she wasn't. I hadn't expected to feel this way about Saitter. After all, if everything went okay, Baton Rouge was about to become my new home.

Daddy's grin fell plumb off his face when he saw me. Then I remembered my haircut. He held out his arms and we hugged. Cars whizzed by and Magnolia stood back a few feet, watching us.

He smiled again, tugging on a short lock of my hair. "Don't worry," he said. "It'll grow back."

When I glanced at Magnolia she was smiling a little.

"Daddy, this is Magnolia."

Daddy removed his hat and held it to his chest. "Nice to meet you, ma'am. Thanks for bringing Tiger home safe."

Magnolia looked confused. "Hmm? Tig—"

"My name is Tiger *Ann*." I said the Ann part real loud, hoping that would be the part to stick.

We rode home, the three of us, side by side in the pickup. This time Magnolia didn't even try to get in the back. She leaned next to the door with her brown elbow hanging out the window. The sun's beams danced between the pine branches and two red cardinals dipped low as they flew across the road in front of us.

"This sure is pretty," Magnolia said, "this place called Saitter."

sixteen

At home, dishes were piled in the sink and covered every square inch of the counters. A bad smell came from Momma's room—a sour smell caused from not taking a bath or changing out of that old gown for over a week. The pulled shades darkened her room, making it even more depressing, and a fly buzzed around Momma's sleeping body.

It was obvious Miz Eula hadn't done a lick of housework, but she didn't keep her own home clean so we couldn't expect her to do anything special to ours. Although she did make three blackberry pies from the blackberries I picked before leaving for Baton Rouge.

"Lawd almighty!" whispered Magnolia, shaking her head, causing her hat to wiggle.

Daddy's ears turned red. "I reckon I should have

done them dishes, but as soon as I'd get home, Corrina wouldn't let me leave her side."

Magnolia stood there with that sack in her hand, the umbrella pointing out at us like an accusing finger.

"Momma isn't always like this," I said. "It's just on account of Granny dying."

"I been paid to do a job," said Magnolia, "and I aim to do it."

My blood perked at the way Magnolia was looking around our house like we were filthy pigs. When Granny was alive our house never smelled or looked like this.

Suddenly I felt shame stab me in the gut. "It's my job to do the dishes anyway. I *aim* to do them directly."

Magnolia pursed her lips and looked me up and down like I was white trash. "Mmm-hmm."

Daddy walked in the bedroom and swatted at a fly. "Corrina," he said gently, stroking his fingers through Momma's hair. "Magnolia is here."

Momma opened her eyes and looked toward the door. Magnolia just stood there. I held my breath, waiting to see what she was going to say about Momma laying there in those smelly sheets.

Instead Magnolia put down her sack and walked

in the room with the biggest smile on her face I'd seen since first meeting her. "Hello, Miss Corrina, I'm Magnolia."

Momma blinked. "Where's Tiger?"

I sprang into the room. "Here I am, Momma. See, I told you I'd be back." I kissed her on the cheek and patted her head. The smell was worse up close. Giant circles of sweat under her arms had stained the nightgown.

"Mister Lonnie," said Magnolia, "it's been a long day. I'm getting tired and fading quick. You mind if I settle in today and start fresh tomorrow?"

I stepped up to her and spoke before Daddy had a chance. "Of course not. Aunt Dorie Kay didn't expect you to start today." My bossy voice surprised me. Magnolia's smile slipped down into a frown.

"Is your name Mister Lonnie?" she asked me.

Daddy started for the door. "I'll take you now if you want."

"That'd be right fine."

My first chance to see the colored quarters and I had to stay with Momma. I headed into the kitchen to wash the dishes.

❀   ❀   ❀

The next morning, when the alarm rang at five-thirty, I hurried to dress for my first day at work. Magnolia was already cooking breakfast in the kitchen. It felt strange to see someone wearing Granny's apron, opening her cabinets, and cooking over her woodstove.

"How did you get here?" I asked.

"And good morning to you too, *Ann,*" she said, stirring a bowl of batter. "I done walked. Ain't nothing but a little piece. Get to see one of the good Lord's miracles that way."

"What miracle?"

"The sunrise. Pinks, purples, oranges. The Lord sure knowed how to bless each day. Your granny knowed how to keep a kitchen. Ain't had to hunt for a thing."

She poured the hotcake batter into the frying pan.

"I like your momma and daddy. They's good people.

"Seems like a girl has everything she want here. A momma and daddy that love her. A fine home, cept'n I'd want a birdhouse or two if it be mine."

I stayed quiet while she flipped golden hotcakes in the skillet.

"Your aunt ain't never home enough to get a man. Why you think she be home for you?"

She was starting to remind me of nosy old Miz

Eula. When I was sure Daddy wasn't in sight, I said, "Aunt Dorie Kay . . . I mean, Aunt Doreen wouldn't have asked me if she didn't want me. Besides, Momma can't take care of me."

"Take care of you? You a big girl. When I's your age my momma laid down and died. The world done wore her out. I had five younger brothers and sisters to take care of and I done it. Your family needs you. Anyway, your momma gonna get out of bed one day soon. You wait and see."

It was almost a relief to hear Daddy announce it was time to leave for the Thompsons'. My stomach fizzed. I hadn't seen Jesse Wade since I told him to leave me alone. There was a good chance I wouldn't see him anyway because he slept late on summer mornings and as long as I'd known him he'd never had much to do with the nursery.

That's what I thought, anyway.

We hadn't taken two steps from the pickup when Jesse Wade ran up to us. His curly hair was flat on one side from where he'd slept on it and his eyes looked puffy. "Morning," he said, bending over with his hands on his knees, trying to catch his breath. When he straightened, he looked at me and his eyes grew as big as a cow's.

My hands flew to my hair.

"Good morning, Jesse Wade," Daddy said. "You're sure up and at 'em early."

Jesse Wade looked at me when he spoke. "Daddy says he could use my help. With the Louisiana Lady camellias and all."

I looked the other way. Otis was dragging a long hose over to a bunch of small camellias planted in a field.

Mr. Thompson drove up in their green car. "Lonnie, you think you can show my son how to do some work here? He hasn't sweated a day in his life, but I think he's capable." Jesse Wade turned red and I felt a twinge of pity for him.

"Yes, sir, Mr. Thompson," said Daddy.

"I'm heading out to Dallas to see that man about the Louisiana Ladies. Be back in a few days. Keep an eye on things for me, will you?"

"Yes, sir, Mr. Thompson. I'd be mighty proud to keep an eye on things."

"Good to see you, Tiger." Mr. Thompson studied me a second, then said, "Tiger, you sure look different for some reason. I guess you're growing up." Mr. Thompson was so excited about those Louisiana Lady camellias, he didn't even realize I'd cut off two feet of my hair. He drove off, kicking up a cloud of red dust as his car sped away.

For a second Jesse Wade and I stood there looking at each other. Then Daddy said, "Well, let's get to work."

Shorty Calhoun and Milton Lambert were leaning against a post when we walked up to them. "Morning," Daddy said, his head lowered.

Shorty snickered. "Lonnie, this is a plant nursery, not a *kiddie* nursery." He poked Milton in the ribs, and they both laughed.

Daddy's ears turned red and he walked away like a boy trying to avoid two bullies. Only I didn't see what was so scary about Shorty Calhoun, who was about an inch shorter than me. And Milton could never catch anybody on account of the polio that had crippled up his left leg. Both men had a reputation for drinking too much on Saturday nights at the Wigwam honky-tonk.

Granny had said Shorty had to spend a night in jail because he cut a man's earlobe off with a broken beer bottle. She'd said, "When that man goes to drinking, he thinks he's six feet tall."

We'd had a good laugh over it then, but today there was something that bothered me in the way he looked at Daddy.

Mrs. Thompson walked up and Shorty and Milton grabbed shovels and starting digging up plants like they'd been working for hours.

"Good morning, Lonnie," she said. "Tiger, I love your haircut. Did you get that done in Baton Rouge?" She put her arm around Jesse Wade. I swear he turned redder than a June strawberry.

"Lonnie, I sure appreciate you showing my son the ropes." She ruffled Jesse Wade's curls.

"Oh, Momma!" said Jesse Wade, stepping away from her reach.

Then she said, "Don't work too hard, *cher*. You know how you tire easily."

I knew Jesse Wade was embarrassed, but I couldn't help wishing I had a momma who would fret and fuss over me.

Daddy started out by showing us how to make cuttings. He picked up some shears and cut six-inch pieces off the older camellia bushes. "These here plants are Mr. Thompson's Louisiana Ladies. So you need to treat 'em *real* special."

After Daddy snipped off a dozen tiny branches, the three of us squatted in front of the sandpile. Daddy poked each cutting upright in the sand, burying more than half of it.

There was nothing to it, and I tried to push down the thought growing in me that Daddy didn't know what he was doing. I was trying to erase the picture of Mr. Thompson finding all these hundreds of little twigs sticking out of the sand and him wondering why the heck he'd been paying Lonnie Parker to work for him.

"Daddy, what are these cuttings supposed to do in this sand?"

He winked and motioned with his finger to follow him down a few rows over. He gently pulled up one of the sticks. Tiny hairlike roots grew at the bottom of the twig. I breathed a sigh of relief.

"Ain't that something?" Daddy said.

Next he showed us how to transplant the cuttings with roots to a bunch of containers made from long boards called liners. The liners were housed in an old shed with no walls so that the plants could receive both sunshine and shade. When those plants matured, workers transferred them into gallon cans and placed them in a hothouse to grow.

"After they get too big for their pots, we transplant them to the field," Daddy explained. He pointed to a cleared piece of ground where Shorty and Milton were planting the young camellias in the soil.

"And that's where they stay until it's time to sell 'em. Then we dig 'em up and wrap their root balls with a piece of burlap." Daddy's hand shaded his eyes and he peered up at the cloudy sky in search of the sun. "Looks like it's lunchtime." Even though he wore his grandfather's watch, Daddy told time by the position of the sun.

"Want to head over to that tree?" Jesse Wade asked me as natural as he had the day Granny, Momma, and I picked purple hulls.

I glanced at Daddy. "Go on," he said. "I'll eat with Otis." Shorty and Milton were already eating, leaning against Shorty's truck. Watching Daddy walk to the other side of the nursery toward Otis reminded me of Magnolia going to the back of the bus. It made me think of what Granny once said, "People are afraid of what's different." I guessed in some ways Momma and Daddy were like Otis and Magnolia and even that colored boy outside the drugstore. They were just too different to some folks.

❦   ❦   ❦

It was awkward sitting there eating lunch with Jesse Wade. I remembered my promise to Aunt Dorie Kay, but somehow my sandwich made my mouth too dry to form the words that it took to say I'm sorry.

Suddenly Jesse Wade pressed his palms against his cheeks, giving his face a squashed-in look. "Please, Mr. Bus Driver, can I come in?"

I looked at him like he'd gone crazy. Then he put his fingers at the corners of his eyes, stretching out his eyelids. "Mommy, Mommy, you made my pony-tail too tight."

I laughed and he looked relieved. "Where'd you learn to do that?" I asked.

"My cousin, Vernon. He said all the kids in Lafayette are doing it. How about this one?" He stuck his finger in his mouth and poked out his right cheek. "Madam, would you kindly remove your umbrella?" The words sounded smothered since his finger was in his mouth.

We laughed until Jesse Wade asked, "Why'd you have to go and cut all your hair off?"

"It's not *all* cut off." I tugged on the ends. "Did your daddy really ask you to work in the nursery?"

He looked down and brushed his hand over the top of the grass blades. It was a rare sight to see dirt under Jesse Wade's fingernails. "Well, he did need the help. And I . . . I thought you'd be here today. I wasn't sure if you'd be mad or not."

"Jesse Wade, I'm sorry that I told you to leave me alone. I guess I felt betrayed when you went to that party without me and I got confused when you acted so . . . mushy."

For about the millionth time that day, Jesse Wade blushed.

"But I want to stay your friend," I said.

He smiled real big. "After all," he said, "we're blood brothers, remember?"

"Yeah, I remember." A few years ago, we'd studied that needle for a good long time, then I finally got the nerve to prick my finger and Jesse Wade went green and said he'd heard you didn't actually have to bleed to be blood brothers. He claimed we could just rub our fingers together and it would give about the same results. There I had sat with blood trickling down my finger and Jesse Wade totally unblemished.

Before long, lunch was over and Jesse Wade and I spent the rest of the afternoon cutting up burlap bags to wrap the plants' root balls. Shorty kept eyeing me like he was trying to scare me. Milton limped along behind him doing anything Shorty did. I guess he was waiting for Shorty to tell him when to jump or laugh at one of his dumb jokes.

At four-thirty Daddy said, "Time to git on home."

When Daddy and I drove up to the house, I noticed laundry hanging out on the line. And there in the middle of my blue jeans and shorts, flapping in the wind, was Momma's nightgown.

seventeen

Daddy and I tiptoed up the front porch steps. We eased open the screen door and took off our shoes.

"Ladies first," Daddy said, holding open the door. I held my breath and walked in.

The smells and sizzles of frying catfish filled our home. The television set was turned off and music poured from the radio. In the kitchen Magnolia dusted cornmeal on a piece of catfish, then dropped it into a black iron pot full of hot oil on the stove. I scanned the room, but Momma's pillow was nowhere in sight.

"Where's Momma?" I asked. Daddy stood right behind me. I could hear him breathing.

Magnolia tilted her head toward the open back door. Momma sat in a chair on the porch with her back to us. She was peeling potatoes into the pea-shelling bowl in her lap. Her long wet strands of hair dripped on her shoulders and Granny's blue night-gown hung loose on her body. I watched her scrape away the skin from a potato in one long spiral. The peeling fell onto the floor and not a speck remained on that potato.

Daddy eased up behind Momma and touched her hair. Without turning around, she dropped the potato in the bowl, grabbed hold of his hand, and leaned her cheek against it, closing her eyes. Just the sight of the two of them together like that made something powerful fill up in me. For a moment I stood there watching them and smelling the sweet air and listening to the frogs croak while the radio softly played in the background.

I tiptoed backward into the kitchen, where Magnolia was slicing an onion. A match stuck out between her teeth. She worked the match over to the corner of her mouth and asked, "Wanna set the table?"

As I put four plates around the table, she said, "Your momma had a nice bath and we got some clean sheets on the bed." I glanced around. The counters and windows sparkled.

"Where'd you get the catfish?" I asked.

"That mailman, Horace. He done dropped a mess of catfish off this morning when he brought the mail."

My stomach did a quick dive. "Horace?" I asked. The thought overwhelmed me—the thought of him showing kindness and the thought of me eating anything Horace had touched.

"He done clean 'em and everything, but I washed 'em again 'cuz I like my food *real* clean. He also delivered a box of baby chicks. I put 'em in the henhouse."

I had forgotten about those chicks. The night before Granny had died, she mentioned that she had ordered them. I felt a strong urge to race out to the chicken yard to see if the gate was closed when suddenly we heard thunder.

"Oh, Lawd!" Magnolia hollered. "All that laundry!"

"I'll fetch it," I said, dropping the forks on the table with a clatter. I dashed out of the kitchen, whizzed past Momma and Daddy on the porch, and arrived at the clothesline just as sprinkles fell from the sky. As I grabbed what I could, I noticed Granny's three sunbonnets hanging together on the line. Only a few weeks ago we wore those bonnets, working side by side in the Thompsons' garden.

When I returned to fetch the rest of the clothes, I

left those bonnets hanging there in the rain as if somehow that could bring back Granny. If only it could, I'd be prouder than anything to stick that silly old bonnet on my head. I'd even wear it in front of Abby Lynn Anders.

As I ran back to the house I glanced toward the chicken yard. The gate was closed.

A half hour later a platter of fried potatoes and catfish lay on the table with a bowl of purple hulls. One plate was missing.

"S'pect I best be getting back," Magnolia said. She held the fourth plate fixed with a serving from each dish.

Daddy caught her as she headed out of the kitchen with her umbrella resting in the crook of her arm. "I'll take you back, Magnolia. No use a-gettin' wet."

"I believe I'll let you," she said. "Now Miz Corrina, I'll not complain if you and Tiger want to do those dishes for me tonight."

Momma looked up at Magnolia with shy eyes— her sparkle missing, but then she gave a little smile and Daddy's shoulders let down like the breath had been knocked out of him.

In Baton Rouge, Magnolia had never let anyone else do chores. Now she was handing out tasks left and right. Maybe she was like Granny, thinking a few chores never hurt anybody. And somehow it seemed like Momma was finding her way back to us just by peeling those potatoes.

When Daddy returned he had a strange look on his face. "Something is a-happenin'."

"What?" I asked.

"Don't know yet."

Fifteen minutes later as the three of us sat together eating, we heard a commotion out front. Daddy and I rushed to the living room window. Hundreds of birds—cardinals, blue jays, bluebirds, sparrows, and robins—had settled in the trees. The birds chirped and tweeted, calling out like they were trying to tell us something important.

Daddy nodded. "Yes, sir, something is a-happenin'."

eighteen

All night I tossed and turned to the sounds of those birds. I tried to sleep with my head under my pillow, but I gave up because I could still hear them. I finally fell asleep by closing my eyes and counting rows and rows of camellia cuttings.

The next morning I awoke to an eerie silence. I got out of bed when I heard Brando scratching at the front door. When I let him in, he darted through the living room and crawled under the couch.

A clanking sound caused me to look out the window. Otis stopped in front of our house in his banged-up truck and Magnolia got out, carrying her umbrella and purse.

I opened the door for her as she was wiping her shoes on the mat. "The sky look like it gonna let loose again," she said.

Daddy walked into the living room and asked, "Have you seen your momma?"

"No, sir."

Magnolia frowned and headed toward the kitchen calling out, "Miz Corrina!"

I poked my head in Granny's bedroom, but Momma wasn't there.

Daddy went out the front door and I ran out the back. We met each other in the middle where Momma was picking butter beans in Granny's garden. Granny's gown had muddy spots over the knees where Momma must have knelt. She was yanking butter beans off the vines and dropping them into a brown sack.

"Corrina," Daddy said, "you better git on out of the mud. The sky's fixin' to do something."

Momma's tongue stuck out of the corner of her mouth like she was concentrating. A strand of hair fell across her face and with a dirty hand, she tucked it behind her ear.

Magnolia hollered from the screened porch, "Did you find that child?"

"She's out here . . . in the garden," I said. "We're trying to get her to come in."

"Leave her be," said Magnolia. I wanted to say,

"What business is it of yours?" But I figured if it weren't for Magnolia, Momma would still be laying in bed, wearing her old stinky nightgown.

Daddy and I went in the house and left Momma in the garden. Thirty minutes later when we headed for work, she was still out there.

On the drive to the Thompsons', I noticed part of the Anders's fence was down again, but we didn't have to shoo their cows off the road. They were out in the field all huddled together, like a bunch of old women gathered around Miz Eula.

Daddy lowered his eyebrows. "Yep," he said. "Them cows know something. So did them birds— the way they all took off."

When we arrived, Milton and Shorty were in the planting field. Milton was picking up the grass and weeds that Shorty had loosened with a hoe. Otis was wrapping burlap around the plants' root balls.

Daddy parked the truck and told me to go over to the hothouse and gather up all the gallon cans I could carry over to the liner shed. "What for?" I asked.

"You'll see," he said, frowning. "I ain't got time to explain more than once." It was the first time Daddy ever sounded impatient with me.

Jesse Wade was nowhere in sight. I figured that his one day of hard work had plumb wore him out. But a second later I noticed he was making cuttings from a Louisiana Lady. He looked so serious, holding those clippers awkwardly in his hands.

Daddy walked up to him. "Jesse Wade, could you go get your momma real quick?"

"Yes, sir." Jesse Wade took off toward his house.

A few moments later he returned with Mrs. Thompson. She wore blue jeans, one of Mr. Thompson's shirts, and his rubber work boots that went up to her knees. "Morning, Lonnie. Anything wrong?"

Daddy cleared his throat. "Miz Thompson. I can't rightly say for sure, but seems like something mighty big is gonna happen with the weather."

"What do you mean?" she asked, peering at the sky.

By then Shorty and Milton had made their way over to us and Otis stood a few yards away. Now everyone was looking at Daddy.

"Well, you see, there was these birds. They landed in our trees yesterday."

"Gee," said Shorty, shifting the wad of tobacco in his mouth. "Birds in a tree, huh? What a mighty strange sight."

Daddy didn't look at Shorty. He kept talking to Mrs. Thompson. "There's millions of 'em. Well, I can't rightly say millions. I didn't count 'em or nothing.

"Them birds, they were hooping and hollering and wouldn't shut up for the life of me. Then this morning, before the sun come up, they just up and left."

Mrs. Thompson frowned. "I don't think I understand what you mean, Lonnie." I felt a blush work its way across my face.

"I reckon them birds know something that we don't," said Daddy.

Shorty interrupted. "Yeah, they know that if they kept it up, they'd have every cat around Saitter after 'em."

Milton snickered and Daddy's ears turned red, but Mrs. Thompson asked, "What do you think it means?"

"I think there's a terrible storm a-comin' this way. Them birds, they knew that. And the Anders's cows do too." The last of Daddy's words faded away.

Mrs. Thompson knitted her eyebrows together. "What about the Anders's cows?"

"They're all huddled up together in the field."

"I've heard of cows doing that before storms," she

said. "Do you think this has anything to do with that hurricane they're expecting toward Cameron?"

Jesse Wade spoke up. "Momma, I bet it does." In that second, watching him stand up for Daddy made me realize all over again why Jesse Wade Thompson was my best buddy.

Shorty stepped forward with the hoe in his hand. "That hurricane's nowhere near here. Saitter might get some rain, but that'll be it."

Mrs. Thompson ignored him. "What do you think we should do, Lonnie?"

Shorty was gripping the hoe so tight his knuckles turned white.

Daddy cleared his throat. "I reckon we should get them Louisiana Ladies safe. Mr. Thompson worked too hard on those camellias to see 'em washed away or beaten to death by the wind."

Shorty looked like he was holding his breath and I saw a vein pop out at his temple. He looked so mad, I was afraid he was going to hit Daddy with that hoe.

Mrs. Thompson stared at the sky. It was dark gray and the clouds had a swept look, but there was no wind and not a drop of rain.

"Okay," Mrs. Thompson said. "Tell us what we have to do."

Shorty took another step closer to Mrs. Thompson. "Don't tell me you're gonna listen to him?" Black tobacco spit sprayed from his mouth with his words.

Mrs. Thompson stepped back. "Of course I am, and you will too if you know what's best for you."

Shorty thumped his finger on his forehead. "But he's *sim-ple!* What would Mr. Thompson say if he knew you were listening to an idiot?"

Mrs. Thompson's face pinched up and she stepped closer to Shorty until her face was inches from his. "Mr. Thompson isn't here and when he isn't here, *I'm* in charge. And I say we listen to Lonnie." Her voice shook a bit, but I could tell she meant what she said. Mr. Thompson sometimes joked about Mrs. Thompson's Cajun temper, but now I wondered if he'd been serious.

"Well, I'll be darned if I'm going to take orders from an idiot or a woman. Next thing I know you'll be asking one of these young'uns how to run things."

"Then you better leave now, Mr. Calhoun."

Shorty threw down the hoe and straightened his hat. "Don't mind if I do. Come on, Milton."

But Milton didn't move. He just stood there looking at the ground.

"If you feel the same way, Milton," said Mrs. Thompson, "you're welcome to leave too."

Shorty clenched his teeth. "Come on, Milton."

Milton picked up the hoe. "I'm sorry, Shorty, but I got a family to feed."

Shorty stared at him a long moment. Milton's crippled leg shook, but he didn't move. Shorty reeled around and stomped off, leaving ruts in the mud where his small boots stepped.

"And don't bother to come back," Mrs. Thompson hollered.

Shorty kept marching away but yelled, "We'll see what Mr. Thompson says about this."

Mrs. Thompson shook her head. She looked at Daddy. "What do we do first?"

"Miz Thompson, if you don't mind your house getting a little dirty, I think that will be the best place for them plants. I figure we can put sheets and newspapers down so we won't mess up your floors. If that wind goes to blowing, those cuttings will take off faster than the dickens. They'll need to be put into buckets. Then I reckon we should take those liners in the house and if there's time, dig up the plants from the field. They might be all right in the ground, but there's no tellin'."

"Let's get busy," Mrs. Thompson said. "I'll lay the newspapers down on the kitchen floor."

Jesse Wade and I followed Daddy to the shed, grabbed a bunch of buckets, and headed to the cutting pile. Otis and Milton started carrying the bigger plants into the house.

"Gentle, gentle," Daddy said when he saw me quickly plucking the cuttings from the sand. "You don't want to hurt the roots. See." He pulled up a cutting like he had the day before, showing me the tiny roots branching out from the bottom of the stem. "They're just like babies."

I slowed my pace, tenderly transplanting the cuttings to the gallon cans. "That's it," he said. "That's mighty fine."

A few minutes later he left Jesse Wade and me to our task and helped the other men carry the larger plants in. After we filled up every bucket, we carried them into the house. Jesse Wade's kitchen and living room turned into hothouses with buckets of camellias everywhere. Milton didn't say a word as he limped along following Daddy's orders, but he didn't have to. His face said it all. It said he was following a fool's orders.

Then we heard it. The wind. It was like a low

whisper blowing against the windows and causing
the tall pine tips to sway and their branches to dance
up and down. Milton's head jerked toward the window and I swear his pale skin went whiter. I wondered what old Shorty thought of Daddy now. But
my pride was quickly replaced by fear.

"Miz Thompson," Daddy said, "if it's okay with
you, I think Tiger better get on home to be with her
momma."

"Of course," she said. "Lonnie, you're free to
go too."

"No, ma'am. Mr. Thompson said for me to keep
an eye on things and that's what I aim to do. There's
plenty of work left here." He turned to me. "Tiger,
don't go the shortcut through them woods. Use the
paved road and hurry."

Jesse Wade looked at me kind of worried. "Want
me to go with you?"

Mrs. Thompson answered for me. "Jesse Wade, I
need you to clear out some space in the bedrooms for
more plants."

I knew Mrs. Thompson was really worried about
Jesse Wade getting out in the storm. I thought of
Momma and what Magnolia had said about family
needing each other.

"Here, Tiger." Mrs. Thompson opened a kitchen drawer and pulled out a yellow scarf. "Tie this scarf around your head and please be careful."

I took off down the road like I was racing the wind. The last thing I expected to see was Miss Astor's calf, Pansy, stuck in the mud on the side of the road, bellowing out for her momma.

Lightning blazed the horizon. Mrs. Thompson's scarf whipped off my head like someone snatched it off, but I caught it before it blew on down the road.

I pushed Pansy's hind end, but I only managed to dig her front legs deeper into the mud. She kept bellowing, sounding more like a lamb than a cow. I stepped into the mud and wrapped my arms around her middle and yanked hard. Three more tugs and she was out. She trotted away from me, heading in the wrong direction.

Why wasn't Abby Lynn out there worried about Pansy instead of me? But I couldn't leave her. Instead of running home, I picked up a stick and tapped on Pansy's behind, chasing her toward the Anders's place. I felt like we were in a Fred Astaire dancing class and Pansy and I were the worst students. She'd head off to the left and I'd run up to her and steer her back to the right.

Finally we reached the fallen part of the fence, where Pansy had escaped. I could see Miss Astor near the Anders's home, standing away from the group of huddled cows in the field. She was calling out to her baby and Pansy was bellowing back. Still I practically had to slap Pansy's hind end all the way up to her momma.

Just as Pansy took off to Miss Astor, I looked up and saw a blur of golden curls by a window. Abby Lynn opened the front door and stepped onto the porch with her hands on her hips. "What are you doing with our cow?" she asked all bossylike.

"Well, I was returning Pansy, but next time I'll let her blow away." Then I added, "In the hurricane."

"What hurricane?" she asked, stepping back behind the door and peeking around it. She squinted. "Say, come here."

I walked up the porch steps.

"Where did you get your hair cut?" she asked.

"I got it cut when I was in Baton Rouge." I could just see an insult itching to get off her tongue.

"It kind of looks like Audrey Hepburn's," she said.

All the times I'd dreamed of being like Audrey Hepburn and it was Abby Lynn, of all people, who thought I looked like her. Or my hairdo anyway.

Suddenly a gust of wind knocked over a rocking chair on the porch. Abby Lynn screamed twice and shut the door without even bothering to say good-bye. In all my years I had never known Abby Lynn to be afraid of anything. I took off running home, but instead of thinking of the hurricane my thoughts were busy with how Abby Lynn thought I kind of looked like Audrey Hepburn. And to my surprise—I didn't care one little-bitty bit.

nineteen

By the time I reached home the wind's whisper turned into a howl, the trees danced faster, and the rain started to pour from the sky. Magnolia stood on the porch, holding the screen door open. Her hair had blown out of its bun and her eyes were opened wide, making her look wild.

"Child, where's your momma?"

"Isn't she with you?"

She shook her head. "When that wind started blowing she done took off like a streak of lightning. She said, 'I gotta go get my baby before the wind blow her away.' Ain't you crossed her path?"

The shortcut. I reeled around and took off toward the woods.

Magnolia hollered something after me but the wind just swallowed her words.

I kept running, Momma's voice drumming in my

ears—*I gotta go get my baby.* Momma had gone after me. Like Miss Astor searching for Pansy. Like Mrs. Thompson keeping Jesse Wade safe at home. Momma had wanted to protect me.

The wind blew and knocked me down twice before I reached the woods. I struggled back to my feet and tore between the trees like they were nothing but tall weeds in a meadow—not minding the scratches I got brushing against them as I ran by. "Momma," I hollered. "Momma, it's Tiger!"

Branches cracked above my head, and I heard them fall to the ground behind me. Mrs. Thompson's scarf flew out of my hand, and I grabbed hold of a pine tree trunk to keep from blowing away. The same thought pounded over and over in my head. If I hadn't wasted time rescuing Pansy and Miss Astor, Momma would be safe at home.

I pressed my cheek against the rough bark while the wind slammed against me and the rain soaked me to the bone.

Then I heard her.

"Tiger."

About a hundred yards to my left, I saw Momma's hands locked around a tree. My heart leaped from my chest. "Momma," I cried, "here I am!"

She inched her way around the thick trunk. She

was barefooted and the wind whipped her wet hair across her face. Granny's drenched nightgown clung to her body like a layer of blue skin. At the same moment we let go of the trees and ran toward each other, the rain pouring down and the wind beating against us. But we didn't care. We just kept running and when we met, we clung to each other as tight and sturdy as those pines. And through the howling of that old wind, I heard Granny's voice whisper to me: *Your momma's love is simple. It flows from her like a quick, easy river.* And for the first time in a long time I felt safe in my momma's arms.

🐛   🐛   🐛

Holding hands, we tried to make our way home through the broken limbs. A few steps out of the woods, the wind knocked us back to the ground. Now I knew why the old-timers called this devil's wind.

Once we got back on our feet, Momma fell. I grabbed her hand and pulled her up. Then I fell. We gave up and crawled in the mud, inching toward the house in slow motion while everything around us moved with great speed. The wind picked up a piece of tin from our chicken house's roof and hurled it toward us. We huddled together with our hands over our heads until we heard it crash to the ground, inches from our feet. Then we started to crawl again. I was glad I wore blue jeans, but I felt sorry for Momma's poor knees. Her nightgown stayed scrunched up at her waist and those knees were being scraped raw. A few yards from the house Magnolia ran from the screen porch and pulled us to our feet, the strength from her small body dragging us the rest of the way. "Come on," she said. "You can make it now."

When we arrived safely inside, baby chicks scattered about the house.

"Oh, Lawd!" Magnolia said. "Those chicks was in a box. That cat must have knocked them over."

I raced after a chick that was heading toward the kitchen. "Why are they in the house?"

"The wind done knocked over the chicken yard gate so me and Miz Corrina put them inside."

We dashed around the house, catching the chicks, which were everywhere—under my bed, in Granny's slippers, next to Momma's pillow. I wondered why Brando wasn't around. I found him under the sofa, his one glowing eye staring back at me. "Brando, you shame your namesake."

An hour later, after the chicks were safe in the box

and we'd cleaned up, Momma and I played Go Fish on the living room floor. Momma's knees were bandaged with clean rags and she wore a loose housedress. Magnolia sat in Granny's chair, reading the Bible, her eyes growing bigger by the second. The wind slapped our house in great gusts, rattling the walls. I couldn't help but tremble.

As I paired up a seven of hearts with a seven of diamonds, I worried about Daddy at the Thompsons'. I hoped he was safe inside their house. He seemed so convinced that he should protect those Louisiana Lady camellias because he had given Mr. Thompson his word.

Magnolia sighed. "This wind is something awful. If I didn't believe in the good book, I'd think—"

Momma ran over to a window, parted the curtains, and pressed her face against the glass. "The wind just plucked our peach tree out of the ground and it's a-headin' toward the Thompsons."

For the first time since she arrived, Magnolia spoke crossly to Momma. "Come away from that window, Corrina."

Momma obeyed, but five minutes later she returned and gave us another update. "Whoops! There went another one of them China trees."

"Get back," Magnolia snapped, stomping her foot.

Momma settled back to her pillow on the floor, but she kept the drapes apart. I saw young trees bend down and touch the ground.

A few moments later when the rain slowed to a gentle patter, Momma's neck stretched toward the window, and the cards dropped from her hand to the floor. "Ma" slipped from her mouth in a whisper, and she suddenly tore out the front door. I heard her feet thump against the porch slabs before I could even stand.

Magnolia dropped her Bible. "In the name of heaven!"

I raced out the door after Momma, but Magnolia's strong grip held my arm and her fingernails pierced my skin. I stood there on the porch helpless, watching Momma try to grab Granny's bonnet that had flown off the clothesline. Momma's dress filled with air like a parachute and her arms reached for the swirling bonnet. Pine needles and oak leaves whirled around her bare feet. "I should have taken those bonnets off the line," I cried. "I shouldn't have left them there."

A gust knocked Momma over, but she jumped back up trying to grasp the bonnet that was spinning just inches from her. Suddenly the wind stopped blowing and howling as if someone flipped off a switch. And just as the world hushed, that bonnet drifted right into Momma's outstretched arms. She held the bonnet to her chest and turned around, smiling. At that minute there was no doubt in my mind that Momma was seeing Granny as clear as I heard Granny's voice earlier in the woods.

"Well, I'll be," Magnolia said, releasing her tight hold around my arm.

Then Daddy drove up in the pickup, jumped out, and rushed to Momma's side. His face was wrinkled with worry, but Momma just kissed him on the lips like he was Marlon Brando. I ran up to them and joined their circle.

"We better get inside," Daddy said. "The wind's gonna head back this way." Together we walked back to the house, Daddy's arms surrounding our shoulders and Momma holding Granny's bonnet to her chest.

A warmth swept over me—mightier than any devil's wind could blow. And despite all the pulled-up trees and broken branches on the ground, I felt my head and heart clear. I was home, and it was exactly where I wanted to be.

twenty

The summer's sun soaked up every trace of rain that Hurricane Audrey brought, but she left her mark anyway. Electricity poles were down and uprooted trees lay scattered in everyone's yards. Miz Eula's front porch was completely swept away, but that gave her tongue something new to wag about for a while.

Our parish lost one life to the hurricane, but Cameron Parish lost hundreds. The fact that Saitter did without electricity for a couple of weeks and had a lot of cleaning up to do seemed like a speck compared to what those people in Cameron went through. The floods came up on them so quick that one man got on the roof of his office building and saw his family float past him.

Our church decided to donate the new piano fund

to a church in Cameron. Even Sister Margaret said, "It's the Christian thing to do."

❀   ❀   ❀

Fall arrived in Saitter like a welcomed spring, and everyone talked about the upcoming party Mr. Thompson was giving for the Louisiana Lady. The whole town was ready to burst by the time the camellia buds opened.

Even Aunt Dorie Kay came up for the big event. It was the first time I had seen her since she took Magnolia back to Baton Rouge. She had been down-right shocked when I told her I wanted to stay in Saitter. The day before she left with Magnolia, we walked down to Saitter Creek and I broke the news. Aunt Dorie Kay frowned. "But you'll be expected to keep an eye on your momma and take care of the household."

"I know," I answered.

Two tiny lines formed between her brows and she straightened her shoulders like she was trying to make herself taller. "Life won't be easy," she snapped.

"I guess I'll take it one step at a time." When I said that, Aunt Dorie Kay shook her head and held my chin for a long moment while her eyes grew misty. Finally she said, "Tiger, you've gone and grown up on me."

Aunt Dorie Kay brought her new boyfriend, Kurt, to the Thompsons' party. They rode from Baton Rouge in his shiny blue Thunderbird. He sure was nice, but with his fish lips and curly blond hair, he didn't look a thing like Elvis.

A reporter with the Alexandria paper came to Thompson's Nursery for the party. He wanted to write an article about the Louisiana Lady, but his attention turned to Daddy when Mr. Thompson told him about Daddy saving the camellias before the hurricane hit.

The reporter tilted back his hat and rubbed his chin with the tip of his ink pen. "So you knew Hurricane Audrey was coming before she hit?"

"Well," Daddy said, "I didn't rightly know it was the hurricane a-comin'. I just knew that something was gonna happen because them birds— they'd been sitting in our trees all night a-carrying on. Them birds knew before anyone. The way I figured it, they was sitting there trying to figure out which way to go. You know like when you got a hankering to go somewhere, but you don't know where?

"Anyway, I told Miz Thompson that we better take care of them Louisiana Ladies before we regret it. On account of all the work Mr. Thompson did.

You know he's worked on this here flower for eight long years. He had the idea way back then and—"

The reporter interrupted. "Getting back to those birds. Is that how you predict the weather?"

"Well, I don't know if you can call it real predictin'. I'm just going on what my daddy taught me. He always said, 'If you listen close enough, the earth talks to you.' "

When the photographer started to take Daddy's picture next to the camellia, Daddy said, "Oh, it wouldn't be right without Mr. Thompson. After all, he's the one who invented the Louisiana Lady."

So the reporter motioned Mr. Thompson into the shot. Then Daddy cleared his throat and said, "It wasn't like I didn't have any help that day. I couldn't have done it without Miz Thompson, and my daughter, Tiger, and Jesse Wade. And of course the other fellers that work in the nursery."

There we all stood, like a big crowd waiting for a parade to march by while the photographer's camera flashed. I saw blue dots the whole day.

After the newspaper reporter and photographer left, we ate dinner on quilts spread on the Thompsons' yard. Momma looked like a pretty sunflower in the yellow dress she had made. She and Aunt Dorie Kay sat side by side, both of them barefooted, drinking from mason jars filled with Momma's extra-sweet lemonade.

Kurt squatted in front of them to take their picture. Right before he said, "Say cheese," Momma slipped her arm around Aunt Dorie Kay like it was the most natural thing to do. I felt something catch in my throat and I was relieved when Jesse Wade ran up to me and said, "Come on. Let's play ball."

It was like old times, only better. This time Dolly, Annette, and Jackie trotted over to the ball field. Abby Lynn sat glued to her momma's side. I had discovered hurricanes weren't the only thing Abby Lynn Anders feared. When school started, she refused to dress out and play baseball during gym class until Coach Masters gave her a direct order. That day when she was up at bat, the kids laughed at her clumsy swings. I reckoned that was why Abby Lynn hadn't wanted to play ball all along. She was afraid of making a fool of herself.

On my way to the field, I moseyed over to Abby Lynn and asked, "Why don't you come play ball with us?"

She batted her eyelashes. "That's okay. I'd rather stay here."

Mrs. Anders nudged her shoulder into Abby Lynn's. "Oh, go on, honey. It'll do you some good."

Abby Lynn frowned at me, but she stood, brushed off her bottom, and followed me to the field. When I looked at her, I recognized something in her face. The "I wish I was invisible" look.

I don't know what came over me. I don't know whether it was the puffed-up pride I had for Daddy about saving the camellias, or the way Momma's arm surrounded Aunt Dorie Kay's shoulders, or just the way the sunshine felt so good soaking my back, but for some reason I felt kind of charitable toward Abby Lynn Anders.

"Abby Lynn," I whispered, "I'm the catcher so when you get up to bat, listen for my voice."

She scrunched up her face at me and I shrugged, thinking, Oh, well. But when her name was called and she got up to home plate to bat, she looked over her shoulder at me. When Bobby Dean pitched his show-off fastball, I watched it spin toward Abby Lynn and waited for the exact moment to say, "Swing!"

Abby Lynn swung the bat and knocked the ball to the ground about three feet in front of her just as Jesse Wade sent me a puzzled look. He was playing shortstop but he didn't move toward the ball like usual. He probably thought there was no reason since Abby Lynn just stood there. She must have thought her hit wasn't any good since the ball only traveled a puny distance.

So I stood and hollered, "Run, Abby Lynn! Run to first base." And for the second time in her life, Abby Lynn actually listened to me and took off for first base.

I cupped my hands over my mouth and called out, "Whooo-wee!"

Jesse Wade threw down his mitt. "You're not even on her team!"

"Yeah!" Bobby Dean yelled from the pitcher's mound. "You're on *our* team."

I smiled and said, "I guess I plumb forgot." I put my fingers to my temples and pulled, making my eyes all slantylike. "Maybe my ponytail's too tight."

Bobby Dean was still fuming, but Jesse Wade's dimples popped out. Watching him smile at me like that made me blush. And at that very moment I felt kind of special knowing that Jesse Wade Thompson gave me my first kiss.

In the distance, the purple hull vines were brown and shriveled in the Thompsons' garden. I squinted, making the garden blurry, trying real hard to see three sunbonnets bobbing up and down between the rows. But it was no use. That day had passed like Hurricane Audrey blowing through Saitter, like Granny dying and Magnolia's visit.

And as I looked to the tall pines reaching toward my Louisiana sky, I reckoned that maybe that's the way life is supposed to be. Some days are like Saitter Creek—smooth and calm, letting you stay a child a little longer, and others are like Hurricane Audrey taking hold of you and spinning you above the pines, making you grow up a little quicker—kind of like cutting your hair on a full-moon day.

About the Author

Seven generations of Kimberly Willis Holt's family were from central Louisiana, and Saitter is based on the small town of Forest Hill. The daughter of a navy chief, Ms. Holt lived all over the world as a child, but Forest Hill became the place she called home. "Forest Hill is the kind of town where neighbors care when you're sick and show up at your door with chicken and dumplings. I wanted Tiger to be from a place like that," says the author.

Ms. Holt has had short fiction published in several literary journals including the *Southern Humanities Review*. She lives in Amarillo, Texas, with her family. This is her first novel for young readers.

GOFISH

KIMBERLY WILLIS HOLT

What did you want to be when you grew up?
A writer

When did you realize you wanted to be a writer?
In seventh grade, three teachers encouraged my writing. That was when I first thought the dream could come true. Before that, I didn't think I could be a writer because I wasn't a great student and I read slowly.

What's your first childhood memory?
Buying an orange Dreamsicle from the ice-cream man. I was two years old.

What's your most embarrassing childhood memory?
In fourth grade, I tried to impress the popular girls that I wanted to be friends with by doing somersaults in front of them. (I never learned to do cartwheels.) They called me a showoff, so I guess it didn't work. If only I'd known how to do a cartwheel.

What was your worst subject in school?
Algebra

What was your first job?
I was in the movies. I popped popcorn at the Westside Cinemas.

How did you celebrate publishing your first book?
I'm sure my family went out to dinner. We always celebrate by eating.

Where do you write your books?
I write several places—a soft, big chair in my bedroom, at a table on my screen porch, or at coffee shops.

Where do you find inspiration for your writing?
Most of the inspiration for my writing comes from moments in my childhood.

Which of your characters is most like you?
I'm a bit like most of them. However, I fashioned Tori in the Piper Reed books after me. But Tori is bossier than I was and she certainly makes better grades than I did.

When you finish a book, who reads it first?
My daughter listens to my read my first draft.

Are you a morning person or a night owl?
I'm a morning person.

What's your idea of the best meal ever?
That's a toss-up. My grandmother's chicken and dumplings, and sushi.

Which do you like better: cats or dogs?
I'm a dog person. I have a poodle named Bronte who is the model for Bruna in the Piper Reed series.

What do you value most in your friends?
Loyalty and honesty

Where do you go for peace and quiet?
Home

Who is your favorite fictional character?
Leroy in *Mister and Me* because he is forgiving. And that's a trait many of us don't have.

What are you most afraid of?
Anything harming my daughter.

What time of the year do you like best?
Fall

What is your favorite TV show?
CBS Sunday Morning

If you were stranded on a desert island, who would you want for company?
My husband and daughter

What's the best advice you have ever received about writing?
A writer once told me, "Readers either see what they read or hear what they read. Writers have to learn to write for both." When I started following that advice, my writing improved.

What do you want readers to remember about your books?
The characters. I want them to seem like real people. I want them to miss them and wonder what happened to them.

What would you do if you ever stopped writing?
I plan on dying with a pen in my hand.

What do you like best about yourself?
I'm honest.

What is your worst habit?
I eat too much.

What do you consider to be your greatest accomplishment?
I gave birth to a wonderful human being.

What do you wish you could do better?
I wish I could do a cartwheel.

What would your readers be most surprised to learn about you?
I send gift cards with positive messages to myself when I order something for me.

What would you do if you inherited the gift that
ruined your father's life? Would you use it?

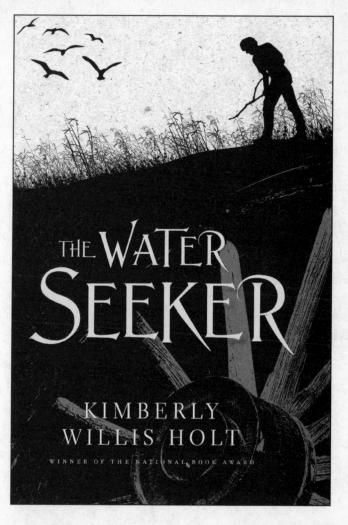

Keep reading for an excerpt from

THE WATER SEEKER

by Kimberly Willis Holt

CHAPTER

1

BITTERSWEET CREEK 1833

JAKE KINCAID WAS KNOWN as the dowser. With a forked branch, he'd made his way from the Arkansas Territory to Missouri, stopping at farms to find water for new wells. His plan was to raise enough money so he could do what he wanted and never pick up the branch again. But the dowsing was a gift. And a gift might be abandoned, but it will always be there, waiting to be claimed.

One farmer didn't have money, so he paid Jake by giving him a parcel of land with a cabin. Since winter was settling in, Jake decided to stay there until spring, when he'd take up trapping. His cabin sat a hundred steps from Bittersweet Creek and about a mile, as the eagle flew, from the Hurd place. When their oldest daughter, Delilah, showed up at his door, begging for a place to stay, he'd not been with a woman in a long time. Without thinking, he said, "Well, I reckon I could marry you."

A few months later, Jake went west to trap. He left each fall and returned in the summer after the trappers' rendezvous. The life suited them. Delilah had a safe haven from her pa's temper, and Jake had someone to come home to. And most satisfying to them both were the months of solitude that they craved.

DELILAH STROLLED through the woods, thinking about how that day felt especially hot. Jake would be making his way from Green Valley, and when he arrived he'd expect a clean house and a hot meal. She hurried home to prepare for him.

Anticipating Jake's arrival always brought on dread and excitement. Every year, Jake traded for supplies with an artist who painted the mountain man's way of life. Delilah looked forward to getting new paints, brushes, and paper. But she also loved her time alone in the woods. And the birds. She loved the birds.

Delilah treasured walking among the pines and cypress trees. She'd grown to appreciate the smell of her own sweat and the way it mixed with the musky smells of the earth. Now she'd have to wash all that away. Jake's return meant she'd have to bathe more often, keep house, and cook meals.

From him, she'd learned how appearances deceived. Her pa, Eb, was a small man who looked as gentle as a cat, while Jake was stocky, barrel-chested, and furry like a bear.

He could talk until the sun fell out of the sky, but Jake didn't have a temper. To Delilah, listening to Jake drone on and on about his trappings was a good trade-off.

A FEW DAYS later, Jake arrived. He grabbed hold of Delilah and pressed his lips against hers. When it seemed he'd never let go, she wiggled free and grabbed his leather satchel in search of the new paints and brushes. She moved so quickly that the bag dropped with a *thump* to the floor, causing a glass to crack. Staring down at it, she could clearly see her own reflection. "What's that there?"

Jake sighed and collapsed upon a chair. "A mirr-o. Was one."

She took off his boots and fed him a bowl of vegetable and bacon soup. Jake gulped down the broth in less time than it took to sneeze. Then he fell asleep.

Delilah carefully set the hand mirror on the table next to her tablet and stared into it. The crack ran the entire length of the mirror, but what she saw fascinated her. She touched her red hair that frizzed like the threads on a ball of wool. When Delilah was a young girl, her ma braided it in a long pigtail and smoothed the wild hairs with lard. Delilah's finger stroked the lines of her nose and her wide chin. She smiled, not just because she was amused, but because she wanted to see what would happen to her face. She had a space next to her black tooth. She'd lost the tooth when Eb punched her for not milking the cow a few years back. Delilah was amazed that a piece of glass could reveal the history of her life. A fire burned inside her, and she began to draw.

IN THE MIDDLE of the night, Delilah heard Jake ease out of bed and pull on his boots. She knew what was next. He did it every summer when he returned. And she knew for sure he thought she didn't know. Last fall, she'd lifted the rock under the oak tree, hunting crickets for fish bait. She discovered the muslin sack buried in the ground under the rock. When she saw the money inside, she fell back on the ground and laughed. Jake didn't know her at all. Money didn't mean a thing in the world to Delilah.

For three months, Delilah cooked and cleaned for Jake, all the while gazing outside the window, praying for cool weather to come. Several weeks before the leaves turned crimson and orange, Jake packed up his mule and headed toward the mountains.

A month later, a sour taste formed in Delilah's mouth and she vomited her breakfast of bread and blackberry jam. Immediately she felt better, but the next morning, the sickness returned. Two months later, her belly began to round out like a melon. She cursed Jake's name to the trees, even threatening to kill him.

Then one November night, as if the heavens had heard her cries, light poured through the cabin window, awakening Delilah from her sleep. She hurried to the porch and discovered streaks of light streaming across the sky. All the stars are falling, thought Delilah. But instead of being afraid, she settled on the top step and watched. There were thousands, too many to count. She just waited and watched. The light was so bright she could clearly see a doe and her young buck in the thick of the woods. The heavens had given her a gift. And hours later, when the shower of light ended, she felt sad.

The next day, Delilah awoke craving bread. Before sunset, she'd baked twelve loaves and eaten three. She tore the other loaves in tiny pieces and scattered them on the porch. In the morning, the birds had discovered her offering. She pushed the table next to the window and began to paint.

By the time winter arrived, Delilah's resentment had disappeared and a softness for the life inside her was growing, though at times she believed they were in conflict with each other. When Delilah curled up in bed to sleep, the baby kicked hard, until she got up and walked the floor. At which time the baby became still. Whenever Delilah settled at the table to draw, the baby caused a burning inside her gut that made her drop the pencil and give up for the day.

She began to dream the same vision each night. In her dreams, she heard a baby cry. Then she saw herself standing by a long winding river. A baby floated by, his little arms stretching toward her. But try as she did, she could not reach him. Downriver, a woman picked up the baby and handed him to another woman. That woman handed him to yet another. And so it went, the baby being passed down through a chain of women along the river. This dream occurred so often, Delilah started to think of it as a premonition. No matter what, she believed her child was destined for trials and tribulations. He would struggle. Delilah was certain of it.

Spring arrived, and Delilah spotted new nests every day. She discovered them in tree branches and corners under the porch cover. She even found one in the hole of the barn wall. The birds crafted their nests from bits of twigs, dead grass, corn husks, and Delilah's hair. She loved seeing her red strands woven in with all the other textures. She always believed she was a part of nature. This was proof of it.

In May, the baby birds began their flight lessons, and a feeling came over Delilah that she, too, was about to spread her wings and take off. She couldn't explain it, but the feeling became stronger each day.

One afternoon, as she walked through the woods, an old blackbird called out to her. *A-mos*, it said. *A-mos, a-mos.* The wind began to howl, but she could still hear the bird's chant. *A-mos, a-mos, a-mos.*

When it was time for her baby, she had no choice but to fetch her ma. She set out for their cabin, walking the mile through the dense woods. Even though it was May, the mornings remained cold. And since there was no worn path, Delilah followed the smell of smoke rising from her parents' chimney. The pain in her womb kept her from noticing the cloud of birds flying above the treetops that towered over her head.

As she'd predicted, her brother Silas was hoeing the garden with Eb.

"I heard you coming the whole way," Eb said. "I could hear those dad-gum birds. They's always following you."

Eb feared birds ever since one swept down and pecked him in the nose. The incident happened three years ago after he'd taken a strike at Delilah. That was the day she took off for Jake's cabin.

A huge flock of crows landed in the garden. Silas removed his hat and waved it overhead as he ran about trying to scare them away. His long, thin limbs caused him to resemble a scarecrow that suddenly came to life. The birds flew away from Silas's reach, circled the garden, then returned.

"Shoo! Shoo!" Silas hollered as he flapped his hat, turning to his right, then his left. He started to spin.

If she'd not been in pain, Delilah would have laughed.

Eb narrowed his eyes at Delilah's stomach. "Looks like you got yourself in a heap of mess, gal."

"I had me a man to help."

Wiping his forehead with his sleeve, he said, "I can see that."

"Jake's my husband."

"I reckon you want your ma. Lolly's in the house." He turned away from her and joined Silas in his crusade, stomping his feet at a group of crows.

Delilah felt the air close up around her. Just returning there had brought back all the bad thoughts. Then Daisy, her seven-year-old sister, ran over and hugged her legs. The girl stared up at Delilah's big stomach and said, "You're as fat as an old grizzly bear."

Delilah stroked her sister's golden red hair. "And you're as tiny as a little squirrel."

Her other siblings acted as if she were a stranger, cowering behind the ladder that led up to the loft. That bothered her most, more than seeing her pa. They've been poisoned against me, she thought. Or maybe they resented her for leaving because Eb had gone to hitting one of them. Her eyes searched each of their faces and arms for bruises, lingering longest on Daisy's. Relieved to discover none, Delilah figured she was probably the lone thorn in her pa's side.

Delilah wanted to return to her cabin for the baby to be born, but Lolly insisted on finishing Eb's dinner first. The sharp pangs came quicker, and Delilah paced on the front porch until Lolly finally joined her. They were making their way through the woods, heading back to the cabin, when Delilah's water broke. Before the sun was down, she was crying out for Jake.

The birds' chatter grew so loud that Lolly hollered, "Them birds are driving me crazy!"

The labor was long and hard, which puzzled Lolly since she'd merely grunted and pushed one time to bring each of her babies into the world. And when Lolly saw more blood coming from Delilah than she'd ever seen with all her own births put together, she suspected the outcome wouldn't be good.

Delilah's screams turned to groans, and her groans became whimpers.

Lolly went outside and found a stick, then gave it to Delilah. "Here, bite down on this."

Delilah yanked the stick from her mouth and flung it across the room. "It tastes like mud."

When the baby finally came, he was red as a ripe raspberry. Wails escaped from his wide mouth as he shook his tiny fists in the air.

Chuckling, Lolly held him up. "This boy is mad." She placed him next to Delilah's breast to suckle. "He's a strong one. What you reckon you'll call him?"

Delilah's lips brushed the light fuzz on his head, and she closed her eyes. Her words came out soft. "Amos is a good name."

"Amos?" Lolly mused. "Where in tarnation did you get that from?"

Delilah didn't answer. She just said, "Tell Jake I done my best. Don't let my baby forget me."

With that, she took her last breath. The cabin and the world outside the window grew silent. And every bird at Bittersweet Creek flew away.